THE SECRET THE
ITALIAN CLAIMS

JENNIE LUCAS

MILLS & BOON

First published in Great Britain 2018
by Mills & Boon, an imprint of HarperCollins*Publishers*
1 London Bridge Street, London, SE1 9GF

Large Print edition 2018

© 2018 Jennie Lucas

ISBN: 978-0-263-07431-4

MIX
Paper from
responsible sources
FSC™ C007454

This book is produced from independently certified
FSC™ paper to ensure responsible forest management.
For more information visit www.harpercollins.co.uk/green.

Printed and bound in Great Britain
by CPI Group (UK) Ltd, Croydon, CR0 4YY

Dear Reader,

What would you do if you had a one-night stand with the man you secretly loved and then found yourself unexpectedly pregnant? You'd tell him, right? But what if, afterwards, that man was so cold and cruel you vowed to raise the baby alone—even though he was a billionaire?

For a year, hotel maid Hallie Hatfield has secretly loved her boss, Cristiano Moretti. When he seduces her it's like a blissful dream—until he tosses her out at midnight and has her fired!

Desperate and pregnant, Hallie is lucky enough to meet two friends at a New York City single moms' group. The three women are very different. Hallie cares most about family. Tess cares about love. Lola cares about money. But they all have one thing in common: they've never told any of the powerful billionaire fathers about their babies.

The Secret the Italian Claims is Hallie's story. Tess's story follows in *The Heir the Prince Secures*. The trilogy will finish with Lola's story, *The Baby the Billionaire Demands*.

I loved writing these stories about three vibrant women and the untameable men who finally meet their match. I hope you love them too.

With warmest wishes,

Jennie

CHAPTER ONE

FAMILY MEANT EVERYTHING to Hallie Hatfield.

Family meant home. It meant being safe and protected even when times were bad. Even when the money ran out at the end of the month. Even when the kitchen cupboards were bare. Family meant always having someone to watch your back, as you watched theirs.

As Hallie had grown up, in an old wooden house built by her great-grandfather, playing in the woods with her brother, learning songs from her mother, tinkering in the garage with her father, she'd known, even as a child, exactly how she wanted her life to be.

Someday she'd get married. She'd raise children, just as her own parents had, without much money but with lots of love. She and her future husband would grow old together, living close to her family, in a cottage with a view of the soft, green Appalachian hills where she'd been born.

Their lives would be full of music and comfort. Because family meant everything.

Then, at nineteen, without warning, Hallie lost everything. Her family. Her home. All the meaning and security in her world.

Now, at twenty-four, the only family she had was the tiny newborn baby in her arms. Living in New York City, she had no job, no money and, as of today, nowhere to go.

But *this* as a solution?

No.

Hallie took a deep, furious breath. "No. Absolutely not."

"But Hallie—"

"Tell my ex-boss about his baby?" Keeping her voice low, not to waken the newborn baby sleeping in her arms, Hallie glared at her friends. "After the way he treated me? Never!"

The other two women looked at each other. The three friends had been introduced months earlier at a single-moms support group, when a mutual acquaintance had realized that all three were pregnant with their first child, and, shockingly, none of them had yet told the fathers.

In Hallie's case, it was for good reason.

Her whole life, she'd tried to see the best in people. To be sympathetic and kind and good.

But she *hated* Cristiano Moretti. After what he'd done, he didn't deserve to know their three-month-old baby existed.

"But he's the father," Tess Foster said gently. A plump, kindly redhead who worked at her uncle's bakery, she cuddled her own tiny baby. "Hallie, you need help. It only makes sense to ask him."

"You're an idiot if you don't get child support," said Lola Price, who was blonde and fiery, and extra-irritable lately—which was saying something—as, unlike the others, she was still heavily pregnant. "Are you an idiot?"

Hallie ground her teeth. That question had already been asked and answered in her own heart. Yes, she'd been an idiot, letting her boss, a billionaire hotel tycoon, seduce her so easily into giving up her long-held dreams of a forever family, a forever home, for one night of passion.

One night? Ha! *Half* a night, since Cristiano had tossed her out of his bed at midnight and then had her fired from her housekeeping job the very next morning!

Who did that?

A selfish bastard with no heart, that was who.

A man who'd ruthlessly thrown her into poverty and homelessness—since she'd also lost her company-paid housing—just because he'd wanted to avoid feeling awkward if he ran into her in the hallway of his hotel.

Hallie looked down at the sweet sleeping baby in her arms. Jack had been over nine pounds at birth, and he'd only gotten chubbier. She loved him with all the ferocious love in her heart. She'd always dreamed of having children. Now Jack was her only dream. Keeping him happy. Keeping him safe.

"You don't even have a place to stay tonight," Tess pointed out. "Unless you're going to call the police on your landlord."

"And you can't stay with me," Lola said, putting her hands over her huge belly. She didn't explain, but then Lola never explained anything.

"I wish you could stay with us, but my aunt and uncle would never allow it," Tess said mournfully. "They're already threatening to kick me out." She sighed. "If only you hadn't ripped up the check your boss stuck in the envelope with your severance pay."

Hallie lifted her chin. "I have my pride."

"But it was for a *hundred thousand dollars*," Tess said.

"And is pride going to feed your baby?" Lola said tartly.

Hallie's shoulders sagged. Lola wasn't sweet and comforting like Tess, but she sure had a way of forcing people to see hard truths.

After her supervisor had fired her, Hallie had stumbled out of the hotel in shock, then opened the severance envelope to discover a check signed by Cristiano personally. As if he thought paying her for taking her virginity would make it all right to toss her out like trash the next morning. Furious and heartbroken, she'd torn it into a million pieces.

Now Hallie realized painfully how that money would have changed her whole life—and Jack's. Because a year later, she had nothing.

But she hadn't known she would end up pregnant. She ran an unsteady hand over her forehead. So much for pride. She would have given anything to have that check back now.

"Come on." Lola stood up abruptly in the middle of the community-hall basement, surrounded by the folding chairs and a crowd of other single moms standing by a punch bowl and cookies that

Tess complained constantly were stale. "We're going."

"Where?"

"To see your baby's father. Right now. It's your only option."

Hallie feared her friend was right. But thinking of facing Cristiano, her courage failed her. "I can't."

"Why?"

"I told you. I was just a notch on the bedpost. He was cruel—"

"Cruel?" Lola's eyes became fiercely protective. "You never said that. What did he do? Hit you? Threaten you?"

"Of course not," Hallie replied, taken aback.

"Then what?"

A lump rose in Hallie's throat. "He ignored me."

The blonde's shoulders relaxed slightly. "He's a jerk. But you're sure he's the father?"

"Yes, but I wish he wasn't!"

Lola's eyes were merciless. "Then make him pay. Child support, if nothing else."

Hallie thought of how desperately she needed money. The lump in her throat became a razor blade. "I can't."

"You don't have any choice. You have no family to help you. Are you seriously going to check into a homeless shelter while your ex lives at a luxury hotel, swilling champagne?"

Hallie sucked in her breath at her friend's frank words.

"And, you never know, he might be happy about the baby when you tell him," argued Tess, who was very tenderhearted. "There might be some perfectly good explanation why he kicked you out that night, then had you fired, then never returned your messages…"

Her voice trailed off. Even Tess couldn't quite overcome how ludicrous it sounded.

If only. Hallie gave her a wistful smile, then the smile slid away.

Tell Cristiano she'd had his baby?

Go back to the luxury hotel where she'd once worked as a housekeeper, to beg for the help of a selfish, ruthless tycoon, and this time give him the opportunity to reject both her and the baby in person? No way.

But looking down at her peacefully slumbering baby, his sweet little mouth pursing in his sleep, she knew Lola was right. Hallie had tried her best to survive on pride. But, after this latest disaster with her landlord today, she had nowhere else to go.

"All right," Hallie said in a small voice.

"You'll do it?" Lola's voice was tinged with relief. For all of the blonde's hard edges, Lola's protectiveness of her friends made Hallie suspect that on the inside she was every bit as kind as Tess but, for some reason, tried desperately to hide it.

"You're right," Hallie said glumly. "I have no choice."

The three of them, plus the two babies and Jack's folding stroller, all piled into a ride-share taxi. But by the time it dropped them off in front of the towering luxury hotel in Midtown, Hallie was already regretting her choice. Just half a night in Cristiano's arms had nearly destroyed her. How could she face him again?

Tess, with her own baby in a comfy sling against her chest, tilted her head back to look at the skyscraper that was the Campania Hotel. "He manages all this?"

"He owns it."

Both women turned to her sharply in the warm July night.

Lola wasn't easily impressed, but her eyes were wide as saucers. "Your ex is *Cristiano Moretti*?"

Hallie felt a little sick as she nodded.

"I thought it was the hotel manager," Tess said in awe.

"It doesn't matter who he is," Lola said fiercely. "Demand what is yours by right. For Jack."

Pushing the stroller, Hallie walked slowly past the neon sign of the Blue Hour glowing in the darkness. The hotel's jazz club had live music, and she'd once dreamed of performing there. Now, as she walked past the club, her failed singing career was the last thing on her mind.

What if Cristiano refused to see her? Or—worse—what if, when he found out about the baby, he demanded parental rights over Jack?

If only she could talk him into just blindly giving her that same big check she'd ripped up the year before!

She stopped, glancing back nervously when she saw her friends following her. "You're coming with me?"

"So you don't back out," Lola said.

"So you don't feel alone," Tess said.

With a deep breath, Hallie squared her shoulders and went through the enormous revolving door into the lobby.

The Campania's lobby was thirty feet high,

gleaming with white marble floors and midcen-
tury-modern furniture scattered around multiple
fireplaces. One side held the long oak check-in
desk, and at the very center of the lobby there
was an elegant bar.

After going inside, Hallie stopped as well-
dressed, wealthy guests passed them by on the
busy summer evening.

"What's the problem?" Lola said.

"Can't you just go to his room?" Tess said.

"No," Hallie said. "There's security. You need
a fingerprint on the elevator."

"Call him, then."

"I don't have his direct number. We never really
talked before…" She hesitated.

Lola scowled. "You were just the hired help,
huh?"

Hallie looked down, her cheeks hot. Even when
she'd worked for him, there were about fifty levels
of supervisors between a maid and the billionaire
owner of an international hotel conglomerate. She
said weakly, "I can try to leave a message with
his secretary, or—"

Her voice cut off with a gasp.

Cristiano had just come out of the elevator on
the second floor, open above the lobby.

The reaction was immediate, as if he were a movie star on the red carpet. Heads turned, people whispered and gasped. His entourage followed in his wake as he made his way down the stairs to the ground floor—a gorgeous, pouting model at his side, with two assistants and a bodyguard trailing behind.

But, for Hallie, everything else became a blur. Even her friends were forgotten.

All she could see was…him.

Cristiano Moretti was broad shouldered, dark and powerful, outwardly civilized in a perfectly cut tuxedo, but with a five-o'clock shadow on his hard jaw and glittering black eyes that hinted at a ruthless, brutal soul. Looking at him, Hallie shivered, caught between longing and fear, overwhelmed by memory of the night he'd seduced her. The night her whole world had changed.

As a trusted maid at the Campania Hotel New York, she'd occasionally been assigned the enviable task of cleaning and tidying the Italian tycoon's exclusive penthouse, used only when he was in town. Dusting pictures of Cristiano's gorgeous face as he stood beside famous politicians and celebrities, Hallie had developed a serious crush. She'd actually imagined that Cristiano wasn't just insanely handsome, he was also honorable and good.

Wrong.

She blinked now, looking at him. The way he smiled. So casual. As if he had not a care in the world. He was so arrogantly handsome, king of the world in his tuxedo, apparently off for a night on the town with a beautiful model. While she'd spent the last year struggling, looking for a new job when she was pregnant and trying to find a cheap place to stay in New York City.

For the last year, he'd been enjoying himself—swilling champagne, as Lola had said. He really had forgotten Hallie even existed.

As Cristiano turned to speak to the woman pouting beside him in a gold lamé minidress, Hallie breathlessly handed the stroller's handle to Lola.

"Keep an eye on Jack."

The blonde frowned. "The man will want to meet his own son."

Hallie set her jaw. "I will tell Cristiano in my own way."

"You're being irrational," Lola began, but Tess put her hand gently on Lola's arm.

"Let Hallie do it."

Hallie flashed the redhead a grateful look.

"Fine," Lola said, drawing back stiffly.

Swallowing hard, Hallie went toward Cristiano, planting herself in the middle of his path through the lobby. Her heart was pounding wildly.

It was funny, really. If she'd known when getting ready for the single-moms group that afternoon that she'd end up facing her old lover, she might have put on lipstick and worn something nicer than an old faded sundress that fit her postpregnancy body. He'd probably take one look at her and wonder how she'd ever ended up in his bed in the first place. Well, there was no help for it now. And it wasn't like she would ever, ever, *ever* want to sleep with him again. Ever.

Putting her hands on her hips, she tried to hide her nervousness as she waited.

His bodyguard tried to smooth his way, holding out his arm. "Excuse us, miss."

Then, from behind him, Cristiano's eyes caught hers.

For a split second, he went completely still. Then his jaw tightened. "It's all right, Luther." He came forward. "What are you doing here, Hallie?"

He remembered her name. She was almost surprised. She hated the shiver that went through her at having him so close, towering over her in his tuxedo, nearly touching her. His dark gaze seared through her. She found herself wanting to blurt out everything, to tell him not just that she'd had his baby but that he'd broken her heart.

She forced herself to say, "I need to talk to you. In private."

His expression became distant. "That's not a good idea."

"I have something important to tell you."

"Tell me now."

"In the middle of the lobby?" Hallie's cheeks went hot. She could feel people watching them. Even the model, standing nearby in her high heels, was looking down at Hallie with scorn. They were all probably wondering why such a frumpy girl would dare talk to Cristiano Moretti. For a moment, Hallie's nerve faltered. She wanted to run away, to forget the whole thing.

Then she saw her friends watching from the other side of the lobby. Saw her sleeping baby cuddled in the stroller. That gave her courage. "It's important."

"Not interested." But as he turned to go, she stepped in front of him.

"Either you speak with me privately right now,"

she said, determined, "or I'll make a scene in this lobby you can't possibly imagine."

Cristiano stared at her for a long moment, as if assessing her. Then he held up his hand, halting the bodyguard's intervention.

"Go ahead to the gala, Natalia," he told his date. "My driver will take you. I'll see you later."

The woman's pout intensified. She glared at Hallie, then said, "All right, darling," and sashayed out of the lobby hips first, as if she were on a catwalk at New York Fashion Week. She was so obviously a model that even the sophisticated patrons of this luxurious hotel turned to watch her go. So did Hallie, a little wistfully. What would it be like to get that much attention wherever you went? *She* would be able to get an audition at the Blue Hour, for one.

"Follow me," Cristiano said, turning on his heel without waiting to see if Hallie followed.

She glanced nervously back at her baby and friends. Then, biting her lip, she went up the sweeping staircase, following the man she hated most on earth, to face him alone in his lair.

Cristiano Moretti's jaw was tight as he went to the wet bar in his private office on the second floor.

Lifting the lid off the crystal decanter, he glanced back at Hallie as she followed him hesitantly into the high-ceilinged room with its dark oak panels. "Scotch?"

Hallie shook her head, her beautiful brown eyes wide.

Turning back to the bar, he poured himself a short glass over ice. He could almost feel her vibrating with anxiety behind him. He put the lid back on the decanter, then drank the Scotch in one long, slow gulp. He realized he was playing for time.

But then, Hallie Hatfield had been Cristiano's biggest mistake. And at thirty-five years old, with his scandalous past, that was saying something.

He turned to face her. *"Va bene,"* he said shortly. "We are alone. What do you want?"

Hallie swallowed, blushed, hesitated. He could see her trying to formulate her words, but she didn't have to say anything. Cristiano already knew why she was here.

She'd come to demand money.

Silently he cursed himself. How could he have been so stupid?

He'd known this would happen. He was just surprised it had taken a year.

Hallie must have spoken with a lawyer who would have pointed out her excellent case for suing him for wrongful termination. His emotions had gotten the better of him the day he'd had her fired, because he'd never done anything so foolish, before or since.

Looking at her, he could almost understand why. Hallie had big, soulful eyes a man could drown in. And her curves! In a loose cotton sundress, her body was even more lush than he remembered. Her dark hair fell in waves over her full breasts, almost down to her tiny waist.

Cristiano could still remember how it had felt to have her in his arms, the sensation of her soft body sliding beneath his as their naked limbs tangled in the very bedsheets she'd made just an hour before.

He'd seduced her. There could be no doubt of that. Coming back to New York a day early, he'd heard her sweet, husky voice singing from the bedroom of his penthouse. Her wistful, heartbreaking melody had filled him with longing for things lost. Things he'd never had. Things he'd never dared even dream of.

Then he'd seen her, waving fresh sheets in the air with her arms spread wide. An incredibly beautiful, sensual brunette with an hourglass figure, leaning over to make his bed. Even that black housekeeping uniform had looked indescribably erotic on her.

A shocked sound had come from the back of his throat. She'd turned and looked at him. A tumble of emotions had cascaded across her beautiful face. Surprise, fear, delight. For a moment their eyes had locked, and he'd forgotten his own name.

Then he'd forced himself to give a casual smile. "You're not my usual housekeeper."

"Camille had to go home early today to be with her grandson, but she warned me not to let you catch me," she stammered. "I'm supposed to be invisible."

Coming forward, his eyes devouring every inch of her, he'd murmured, "You're anything but invisible. What were you singing?"

"Just an Appalachian folk song."

"It's beautiful." Coming close enough to touch her, he'd whispered, "So are you."

Her cheeks had gone rosy, her lips parting in unconscious invitation as she stood beside his enormous bed.

He'd reached for her.

Cristiano knew who was at fault. He'd wanted

her. So he'd taken her. Without thinking of the consequences. If he had, he would have stopped himself. It was one of his rules: never sleep with employees.

But that wasn't the worst rule he'd broken. Hallie wasn't just an employee. She'd also been a virgin. Virgins were off-limits. He didn't toy with women who might mistake sex for love and become a problem later.

He'd known she was a virgin from the first time he'd kissed her, when he'd felt the tremble of her sweet lips. He'd felt her hesitation, her shyness, her inexperience. And he'd known. Somehow, this incredible woman was untouched.

It hadn't made him stop. He was a man who put few limits on his own behavior. But he had a code of honor. In Hallie Hatfield's case, he'd recklessly blown through his own rules like dynamite through a brick wall.

So it was no wonder he'd broken a third rule, afterward, and fired her for sleeping with him.

That wasn't the reason he'd given her supervisor, the head housekeeper, of course. But it had been obvious to Hallie. And clearly her lawyer, too.

But now, as Hallie stood across from him in

his private office, biting her full, delectable lower lip, it was hard for him to think about lawyers when all he wanted to do was pull her back into his arms.

For a year, he'd done his best to forget her. He'd told himself he had. Now he knew that was a lie.

"Why are you here?" Cristiano demanded in a low voice.

"I came to…came to tell you…"

Her husky voice trembled, stopped. She looked at him.

Turning away, Cristiano set down the crystal lowball glass heavily on the dark wood bar. He clenched his hands at his sides to keep himself from the temptation of pulling her into his arms and kissing her to see if her lips were still as delicious as he remembered. He was drawn by the sweet sin of her mouth. Of her body. Of her deep brown eyes, luring him into their depths.

Possessing her once had not been enough. After he'd had her that night, he'd just wanted more. It didn't help that, naked and soft in his arms, she'd looked up at him in bed as if she were half in love with him already. She'd lured him like a siren to give him more than just his body. More than just his money.

But sex and money were all he could give any woman.

So he'd sent her away, tossing her from the warmth of his bed when his body was still aching for more. After she'd gone, he'd still longed for her, like a sweet, forbidden poison. First thing the next morning, he'd contacted her supervisor and arranged to have her fired. For her own good. And his.

But he had never stopped wanting her. And now, as he stepped toward her, his breathing was hard. And not just his breathing.

"Tell me what you want."

"I need to tell you something. Important."

"So you said." Cristiano's voice was low as he looked down at her. He came closer, almost close enough to touch her. His mind was scrambling for rationalizations as to why he should.

Perhaps if he slept with her just one more time…

Got her out of his system…

Stop, he told himself furiously.

Hesitating, Hallie licked her full, pink lips. He nearly groaned. Was she purposely taunting him?

"This…isn't easy to say," she whispered.

Gritting his teeth, he glared at her. "Let me say it for you, then. I already know why you're here."

Her caramel-brown eyes went wide.

"You know?"

He set his jaw. "You never cashed the check."

Hallie blinked, furrowing her forehead. "The check?"

"The morning after."

Her cheeks colored and she looked away.

"No," she said in a low voice. "I ripped it into a million pieces and threw it in the trash."

"Because you knew, even then, you could demand far more."

Hallie looked at him sharply.

"I can?" she whispered. "You'd give me money, just for asking? Why?"

"You want me to admit it aloud?" He pulled her roughly against him. She gasped as his hands suddenly moved over her waist, her hips.

"What are you doing?"

"Checking for a microphone." But even through the thin cotton of her sundress, touching her waist and hips without crushing her lips with his own felt like torture.

"Let me go," she breathed, not moving.

He released her. Stepping back, he leaned against the marble fireplace, folding his arms and keeping his voice very cold. "Who is your lawyer?"

"My lawyer?"

"Don't try to pretend you don't have one. You knew I'd want to keep this quiet. I'm not proud of it."

Her eyes widened. "Of—of what?"

"It would hardly improve the public image of my company if the CEO is sued for sexual harassment."

"Oh." Biting her lip, she looked away, staring for a long moment at the wall of leather-bound books he never read, and the leather reading chair he never sat in, both brought in by an interior designer to make his office look like a nineteenth-century gentleman's study. And all Cristiano could think right now was that he wanted to bend her back against the enormous dark wood desk, kiss her senseless, pull off her clothes and…

He had to get rid of her before he did something else he'd regret.

"Just tell me the amount," he said tightly.

"The amount?"

"How much?"

Licking her lips, Hallie said, "I want…the same amount as before."

"A hundred thousand dollars?" he said incredulously.

"I'll never bother you again. I give you my word."

Cristiano could hardly believe she'd ask for so little. Far less than he'd pay if they went to trial. Less than he paid his lawyers for a month. Was it some kind of trick? Or had she been given bad advice by the worst lawyer in the world?

Searching her face, he warned, "You'd have to sign a nondisclosure form."

"I'll sign anything you want," she said meekly, folding her hands in front of her like a nun at prayer.

Now Cristiano was really suspicious. "And a statement admitting that you were fired for cause."

"What does that mean?"

"You'd say it was your own fault you were fired." He gave a careless shrug, even as he watched her closely. "The reason can be anything you want. Tardiness. Stealing."

"Stealing!" Hallie repeated indignantly. Then her expression deliberately smoothed over and became meek again. "I will admit to being late. Yes. I was very, very late."

Something in Hallie's tone when she said *I*

was very, very late rang true. And yet he knew it was not.

The morning Cristiano had decided to fire her, he'd asked the HR department to review her file, hoping to hear a legitimate reason she deserved to be let go. "Oh, no, sir," the HR head had chirped. "Miss Hatfield is one of our hardest-working employees. She works late and volunteers to work holidays instead of employees with kids. And she's never late!"

So he'd given the task of firing her to her supervisor, instead. Handing the head housekeeper a sealed envelope with a big check, he'd explained to the woman that he'd found Hallie intrusive and her singing annoying. The head housekeeper, whom Cristiano had never spoken to directly before, hadn't asked the same questions HR would have. She'd just followed his order.

So why would Hallie accept a hundred thousand dollars now, in lieu of a settlement that could have brought her millions? And want it so badly she was actually willing to defame her own character for it?

What kind of incompetent, useless lawyer would ever advise her to do such a thing?

Cristiano could barely restrain himself from

telling her what a bad deal she was making. But his goal was to be rid of her before she caused him any more damage—personally or professionally.

"Fine." He turned to his enormous desk. Pulling out a standard nondisclosure agreement usually given to high-level executives, he pushed it across the desk toward her and scribbled something on a separate piece of paper.

"Might as well keep the lawyers out of it, and save us both time and trouble," he said carelessly. "Sign these and I'll write you a check."

Hallie looked at him sharply. "Give me the check first."

"What?" He gave a low laugh. "You don't trust me?"

"No." She looked at him with quiet determination. "Because I know what kind of man you really are."

His back snapped straight. "What kind is that?"

"You seduced me—" her dark eyes glittered in the shadows "—then had me fired. You took my job away, just to avoid the inconvenience of seeing me."

She was right. And he hated her for it.

"And now we both know what kind of woman *you* are," he said coldly. "The kind of woman who is willing to lie about herself for a hundred thousand dollars."

Her deep brown eyes held his, then dropped.

"Yes," she said in a low voice. "I suppose I am." She squared her shoulders. "But I'll still need the check before I sign."

"Fine." Turning away, he got his checkbook out of the safe. Scribbling the amount and signing it, he handed it to her.

Her hand trembled as she took the check. For a moment, she just looked down at it. Then she pressed it against her chest, looking almost near tears.

"Thank you," she whispered. "You don't know what this will mean to us."

"Us?"

"Me," she said quickly.

Obviously, she'd already found another lover. The thought bothered him. He pushed it aside. He had no claim on her, and she would have none on him once the deal was finished.

Setting his jaw, he held out the pen. "Now your side of the bargain."

"Of course." Taking the pen, she leaned over his desk to read the two documents—the nondisclosure agreement and an admission of fault. As she read, Cristiano's gaze traced unwillingly down her long throat to the dark hair tumbling down her back to the sweet fullness of her backside. Her breasts seemed fuller than he remembered.

He forced himself to look away.

Signing both papers with a flourish, she put the lid back on his pen, then handed it to him along with the signed papers. "Here."

She seemed strangely joyful, as if the weight of the world had just been lifted off her shoulders.

Cristiano barely restrained a scowl. His hand brushed hers as he took the papers and pen. Her cheeks went bright red, and she dropped her hand. "Thanks. Goodbye."

He watched incredulously as, without another word, she headed for the door.

"That's it?"

Hallie glanced back with a smile. "You wanted to be rid of me."

He couldn't believe it could be so easy for her to leave him when it was so hard for him to let her go. When it took all his self-control not to ask her to—

"Stay for a drink," he heard himself say. "Just one drink. To toast the future."

The corners of her lips curved into a humorless smile. "Isn't Natalia waiting for you?"

"Who?"

"Who?" She snorted. "The gorgeous supermodel you were taking out tonight."

"She's just a friend," he said impatiently. He knew the Russian girl wanted more. But what did he care about her? Seeing Hallie today had brought back everything he'd tried to forget over the past year, everything he knew was forbidden but that he still wanted. "Share a drink with me."

For a second, Hallie hesitated. Then she straightened, glaring at him. "After the way you treated me, do you really think I would ever choose to spend more time with you?" She lifted her chin. "I never, ever want to see you again. Goodbye, Cristiano."

She turned away, clutching the check against her heart. She left him without looking back.

Cristiano stood in his private office, stunned.

Hallie would cause no legal trouble. The cost of his night with her had been minimal, one he'd been more than willing to pay. And now she was gone. For good.

His jaw tightened. It was what he'd wanted, wasn't it? He'd wanted to permanently rid himself of the temptation she offered. He'd never felt so attracted to anyone.

He'd slept with beautiful women before. The danger—the difference—was in Hallie's voice, so rich with heartbreak and longing. And in her deep brown eyes, which had looked at him with such frank joy. In her low, husky laugh that had melted him with her warmth and delight.

She'd made him feel things against his will.

Not with his body.

His soul.

So after he'd fired her he'd ordered his secretary to block Hallie's calls if she ever tried to contact him again.

Yet, tonight, he'd been the one who had asked her to stay. And Hallie, without any apparent difficulty or regret, had gotten what she'd wanted and easily walked away.

His pride was in shock.

As a matter of course, Cristiano always put his own selfish desires first. You had to look out for number one.

He'd just never imagined a kindhearted country girl like Hallie could do the same.

Rubbing the back of his head, he put his checkbook back in the safe. He told himself he'd go meet Natalia and spend the evening at yet another bland charity gala, but the thought seemed ridiculous.

Hallie had looked delicious, her body even more curvaceous than he remembered. She had a new maturity about her. Her dark eyes had become guarded, he realized. Not as honest and clear as he remembered. She'd held something back. Some mystery. Some secret.

Cristiano closed the safe, then stopped.

Something didn't make sense.

When Hallie had first met him in the lobby, she'd been nervous and tense. *I have something important to tell you*, she'd said. But what was it? Simply that she'd hired a lawyer?

Except she'd never actually said that. Cristiano had. She'd been slow to talk and so he'd filled in all the blanks. When he'd offered her money, she'd been surprised, even shocked. Surely that was why she'd asked to speak to him privately. Because her lawyer had told her to.

Unless she didn't actually have a lawyer.

Unless she'd come to him for some other reason. A reason she'd decided to forget once he'd offered her a check.

Cristiano's eyes widened.

He strode out of his private office and down the sweeping stairs that overlooked the huge, gleaming lobby with enormous chandeliers hanging from thirty-foot ceilings. His eyes scanned over the crowd of wealthy tycoons and beautiful starlets that filled the lobby and main bar of the Campania on a typical Thursday night.

He saw Hallie on the other side of the lobby, near the door, talking to two young women, a plump redhead and a pregnant blonde. Hallie smiled, her joy obvious even from this distance, as she reached out to take something from the blonde.

A baby stroller. Looking down at it, she smiled and cooed.

Cristiano's blood went cold.

A baby stroller.

A baby.

Later, he wouldn't even remember how he had reached her. His brain was blank, his body like ice as he walked through the faceless crowd toward Hallie Hatfield and the baby stroller she gripped by the handle. When he drew close, he heard her soft laughter as she turned to her friends. The other women's eyes went wide as Cristiano put his hand on her shoulder.

Hallie's face was still smiling as she turned. Then the blood drained from her face.

Cristiano looked from her guilt-stricken face down to the small, dark-haired, fat-cheeked baby drowsing in the stroller. He slowly lifted his eyes back to hers.

"Is this your baby, Hallie?"

The fear in her eyes told him everything he needed to know.

The other two women stared between them, wide-eyed.

"You didn't tell him?" the blonde said.

"Oh, Hallie," the redhead whispered.

"Please, just go," Hallie choked out to them. "I'll call you later."

The blonde looked like she intended to argue, until the redhead tugged on her arm and drew her away.

Standing alone with Cristiano in the crowded lobby of his flagship hotel, Hallie took a deep breath. "I can explain."

Cristiano looked back down at the baby. A baby with dark eyes exactly like his own. Suddenly he knew exactly why Hallie had come here today. And exactly why she'd changed her mind.

He controlled his voice with effort. "You have a baby."

She bit her lip. "Yes."

He lifted his cold gaze to hers. "Who is the father?"

Hallie said pleadingly, "Please, Cristiano, don't…"

"Who, damn you."

She flinched. When she spoke, her voice could barely be heard over the noise of the lobby. "You."

That single word exploded through him like a grenade.

He had a child?

Heart pounding, Cristiano looked at the tiny, yawning baby. Emotions rose, choking him. Savagely repressing his feelings, he looked at her.

"You are sure?" he said flatly.

"Yes," Hallie replied in the same tone. "You know I was a virgin when—"

"I know," he bit out. "But perhaps after…"

"You think I rushed into bed with someone else after that?" Her expression tightened. "You are the only man I've ever been with. Jack is your son."

He had a child? A son?

His name was Jack?

Cristiano's throat tightened. "Why didn't you tell me you were pregnant?"

"I tried." Hallie's beautiful caramel-brown eyes narrowed. "I left two messages with your secretary."

Cristiano hadn't gotten those messages because he'd told his secretary never to tell him if Hallie called.

But he didn't want to hear reasons he might be at fault. He wanted to blame only her. "We used protection," he said accusingly. "How did this happen?"

She raised her eyebrows. "You are the one with all the experience. You tell me."

He ground his teeth. "You should have tried harder to contact me."

"After the way you treated me," she said, "I shouldn't have tried at all. Why give you the chance to reject our baby like you rejected me?"

His shoulders tightened as her shot hit home.

"So you were just going to walk out of here tonight." His voice had a hard edge. His throat felt raw. "Once you had my check, you had no reason to tell me about my child. You were going to keep him a secret from me for the rest of my life, weren't you?"

Not meeting his eyes, Hallie gave an unsteady nod.

His hands clenched at his sides. "Why?"

"I've never known what it was to hate someone, Cristiano," she whispered. She lifted her gaze to his. "Not until you."

He was shocked by the fury and hurt he saw in her eyes. "I could not have hurt you that badly," he ground out. "We barely knew each other."

"You were so seductive. So tender. You made me think you cared, just a little." She ran an unsteady hand over her forehead. "But as soon as you got what you wanted, you showed me it was all a lie. You left me jobless, homeless. Pregnant and alone. I gave birth alone. I took care of him alone. Do you know how hard it is to look for a job when you have a newborn? I struggled to put a roof over Jack's head while you pretended we didn't exist." She looked around the luxurious lobby. "While you drank champagne and went to parties."

Her words made him feel oddly guilty. He didn't like it. "You never told me—"

"I came here to beg you for money, Cristiano."

Her beautiful brown eyes were suddenly luminous. "To *beg*, so I wouldn't have to stay at a homeless shelter tonight. Can you imagine how that feels, asking someone you hate for help?"

No. Cristiano couldn't imagine lowering his pride to such an extent. Even when he'd been orphaned in Italy, desperately poor, he would have starved before he'd have done it.

But women were different, he told himself firmly. They didn't have the same fierce pride as a man.

"Then I offered you the check," he said, "and you decided to take the money and run."

"I'm doing you a favor," she said vehemently. "It's not like you'd want to be a father. So just forget I came here. Forget he was ever born."

Turning, Hallie started pushing the stroller away.

As he watched them go, the hotel's marble floor became suddenly unsteady beneath Cristiano's feet.

A flash went through him, memories of when he was six, when he was ten, of being dragged from one sagging apartment to the next, based on the preference of whichever useless new man his drunken mother had taken as her latest lover.

He'd felt helpless as a child, lonely, never staying in one school long enough to make friends.

Most of the household's scant money had gone to alcohol. There had been very little for food and none for Cristiano's clothes, which the local priest quietly donated.

He'd never had a father, unless you counted Luigi Bennato, whom Cristiano assuredly did not. He'd never had a father to look out for him or protect him, even as a baby.

Without thinking, Cristiano stepped forward and grabbed Hallie's shoulder.

"I won't let you do this," he said hoarsely. "I won't let you take our baby away."

"Why?" she said scornfully. "Because you want to be a father?" Her eyes glittered. "Don't make me laugh. You're a selfish playboy, Cristiano. An indecent excuse for a man. You couldn't love someone if you tried, not even your own child. And now that I have enough money to support my baby, I don't want any part of you."

CHAPTER TWO

STANDING IN THE hotel's glamorous lobby with her arms folded, Hallie glared up at Cristiano as if she weren't in the least afraid. But the truth was her whole body was trembling with the effort it took to defy him.

She wished she'd followed her initial impulse when Cristiano had first come into the lobby, and turned and run.

But he'd have caught up with her before she'd even made it out the hotel's revolving door. A single glance at his supremely masculine, muscular body and the cold ruthlessness in his hard gaze was enough to tell her that.

Everything about Cristiano was dark, Hallie thought with a shiver. Dark hair. Dark eyes. Dark tuxedo. A five-o'clock shadow that stroked his hard cheekbones to the slash of his jawline and, most of all, his dark fury as he came closer to her, his hand still on her shoulder, his hulking body almost threatening.

"So this is what you think of me." His black eyes narrowed to slits. "That I'd coldly write you a check and abandon my child to your care."

She was quivering but refused to be cowed. "Money is all you could ever offer as a father. Why don't you just admit it?"

His grip on her shoulder tightened. "You lie to me, you take my money. Then you insult me to my face?"

He had a point, which made her want to throw the check back in that face. Her hand was already rising to do it when she remembered Lola's harsh words. *"Is pride going to feed your baby?"*

With an intake of breath, Hallie clutched the check more tightly. This money would be her baby's security and hope for the future. It would also give Hallie a chance to finally give up her stupid dream of becoming a singer and let her train for a real job, like an accountant or a nurse.

She wasn't going to let pride ruin her life. Not anymore.

Or Cristiano Moretti.

"You should thank me," she said.

He grew very still. "*Thank* you?"

"We both know, whatever you might say now,

that you couldn't truly commit to anyone, even a child."

"How do you know?" he ground out.

"You, commit? For a lifetime?" She gave a choked laugh. "You couldn't even commit for a *night*." She tilted her head. "Were you that quickly bored, the night we were together? Or did you have another date afterward?"

His expression changed infinitesimally. "You think I sent you away because I was bored with you?"

Hallie thought of the glamorous supermodel she'd just seen on his arm. "What else?"

She couldn't let him see how badly that hurt her. When he'd first taken her in his arms that romantic night, she'd been so naive. She'd thought it was fate, an irresistible force drawing them together. She'd thought it was magic.

Hallie had been startled when he'd walked into his penthouse early that afternoon. She'd been warned to be invisible and that her cleaning must be spotless. After spending so much time dusting pictures of his handsome face, seeing Cristiano in the flesh had shocked her.

Cristiano Moretti was a dream come to life. A

famous playboy, the self-made Italian hotel billionaire who dated princesses and heiresses.

And inexplicably, he'd wanted *her*.

One moment she and Cristiano had been talking by the bed; the next she'd been in his arms. After so many bleak years of anguish after losing her family and her home, when her handsome billionaire boss had lowered his lips to hers, Hallie had imagined all the pain was behind her. She'd thought her life had just changed for the better.

And it had, in one way: her baby. Jack was all that mattered now.

"I'm leaving," Hallie said defiantly. "Once I cash your check, I promise you, we'll be gone for good."

Cristiano lowered his head until it was inches from hers. "And I promise you. You'll do nothing of the kind."

Her mouth went dry. As their eyes locked, her heart pounded in her throat as she realized her stupid, idiotic mistake.

She never should have openly defied Cristiano. Because he'd taken her words not just as a challenge but as an insult to his masculinity. To his honor, even.

All this time she'd been thinking about her

pride. She hadn't considered his. And now he would make her pay for it.

"You don't want me," she whispered, her voice almost pleading. "You know you don't."

His dark eyes seemed like deep, fathomless pools as his gaze ripped into her soul. Then he straightened.

"You're wrong about that. I've wanted you for a year. And now I will have you."

"What are you talking about?"

His gaze fell to the stroller and his expression grew cold. "He's my child, Hallie. I'm not going to let him go." He focused on her. "Or you."

"I won't be your mistress, if that's what you mean," she said, struggling to keep her voice calm, not to show her rising fear.

"I know." Cristiano's black eyes suddenly glittered, and he smiled. "Because you're going to be my wife."

His wife.

Cristiano watched Hallie's eyes widen in shock.

It was strange, he thought. He hadn't known he was going to demand marriage until the words came out of his mouth. His whole life, he'd never once been tempted to marry. Of course he'd never imagined he'd be a father, either. And as he spoke the words, he suddenly realized he did want to marry her.

Call him an indecent excuse for a man?

Say he was incapable of committing for longer than a night?

Tell him he couldn't even love his child if he tried?

No.

Cristiano wouldn't abandon his newborn son to endure the same helpless childhood he'd known. Not when he himself had spent most of his adult life seeking vengeance on the father who'd abandoned him before he was born.

But he couldn't wrench his son away from Hallie, either. Mother and child were obviously bonded. Still, he needed to take control of the situation.

Marriage was the brutally simple solution.

"Marry you?" Hallie choked out, searching his gaze as if waiting for the punchline. "Are you crazy? I told you—I hate you!"

"And I'm none too fond of you." But as he put both hands on her shoulders and looked down at her, his nerve endings sizzled from the contact.

He might be angry, but he'd told her the truth. He hadn't stopped wanting her for a year.

Her gaze fell unwillingly on his lips before she glared up defiantly. "Why would I marry you?"

Looking down at the baby, who was now awake and trying to grab his own feet in the stroller, he said quietly, "For our child."

"But...you can't seriously want to be a real father." There was a new nervousness in her voice. "If you want to see Jack, maybe we could talk about visitation—"

"No," he said coldly. Her expression looked relieved until he continued grimly, "I will have full-time, permanent custody."

Hallie's beautiful face blanched. She whispered, "You'd try to take him from me?"

"No." He gave her a cold smile. "I want him to have two parents. Even though you didn't care about that."

Patrons and staff in the lobby had been staring at them for a while, but now they were coming closer, obviously trying to listen.

"I'm not having this conversation here," he said abruptly. "Come with me now."

She glanced around wildly, and he wondered if she was actually considering trying to flee. To help her avoid the temptation, he gently lifted the baby from the stroller.

"What are you doing?" she gasped.

"Holding my son," he said, and started walking. She immediately followed him to the elevator, as he'd known she would.

"Want me to come up with you, Mr. Moretti?" his bodyguard asked.

Cristiano shook his head. "Tell Natalia I won't be able to attend the gala after all. Give her my apologies."

"Sure, boss."

Cristiano continued into the elevator, with Hallie's stroller dogging his heels. Once inside, he pressed his fingerprint against the hidden button for the penthouse.

As they rode the elevator to the top floor, she watched him anxiously. He tried to act casual, as if he'd held a baby before, but he felt awkward. Even three-month-old Jack seemed to be looking up at him in disbelief, as if trying to decide whether to cry or not.

"You're doing it wrong. Hold his head like this," Hallie blurted out, positioning the baby differently in his arms. She shook her head impatiently. "Just give him to me."

"Forget it," he said crisply. Jack was his son and, in some respects, until he secured her loyalty as his wife, Hallie was his enemy. There was no way he'd admit he didn't know what he was doing or give the baby back to her care in a sign of weakness and surrender.

The elevator door slid open onto a small hallway with a grand door and a smaller, inconspicuous one farther down. The top floor of the Campania Hotel was devoted exclusively to Cristiano's penthouse and terraces, with a small separate apartment for his bodyguard. He had a similar penthouse in his flagship hotel in Rome and smaller private suites in his hotels in Tokyo, Sydney, Rio, London and Berlin. He could have rented out the space to paying guests when he was away for an exorbitant amount, but he kept them to himself. Life was about little indulgences, or what was the point of being rich? A man, particularly a wealthy playboy, needed privacy.

Hallie followed him anxiously into the penthouse, as if she feared he might drop the baby. It was insulting. Especially as Jack gave a soft whimper in Cristiano's arms.

"Give him to me—now!" Hallie said.

Keeping his expression inscrutable and moving

with deliberate slowness to show her that he was doing it as his own decision, not hers, he carefully handed her their son. Leaving the stroller in the foyer, she clung to the newborn as if they'd been separated for days.

"You bastard," she choked out. "Dragging us up here. It's practically kidnapping."

"Kidnapping?" He looked down at her coldly. "How about trying to steal my son from me for the rest of my life?"

Some of the anger in her gaze faded. "If you cared so much, you should have taken my calls when I was pregnant!"

He hated that she was right. With a low, bitter laugh, he turned away. "You remember your way around, I presume?"

She followed him into the enormous room with its starkly modern furniture and floor-to-ceiling windows that offered a magnificent view of the city's sparkling lights. To the left, an open-concept kitchen had all the latest appliances, none of which he'd ever used. There was a reason he chose to live in his own hotels.

He looked back at her. Hallie's cheeks were pink. He wondered if she was remembering when she'd cleaned here, as the maid. Or if she was remembering, instead, the night she'd helped him mess everything up again, tangling the bedsheets in a night of passion so hot it had burned past all barriers to create a child. A night he could never forget.

"Have a seat," he said coolly even as he fought the flash of heat at the memory. He indicated the white sofa that overlooked the spectacular view.

She tossed her head. "No, thanks. I don't intend to be here long enough to—"

"Sit down," he said more forcefully, and glaring at him, she obeyed, cradling the fussing baby in her arms.

Cristiano sat down in the white chair beside the sofa. He didn't need to see the city view; he knew it so well by now it bored him. He looked only at her.

"If Jack is truly my son, he belongs with me."

She set her jaw. "You're only saying that because I insulted your pride. You don't really care about him."

He narrowed his eyes. "Oh, you know that, do you? Because I'm an indecent excuse for a man? Because I couldn't love someone if I tried?"

She had the decency to blush. "I'm sorry if that was rude. But it's true."

He restrained himself from tossing a few insults back in her face, insults she richly deserved. "You don't trust me? Fine. I don't trust you, either." He looked down at the baby in her arms. "So from now on, my son is staying here."

"No."

"I will not allow him to disappear from my life just on your word that you'll take good care of him."

"And I won't let you turn our lives upside down, just because I injured your masculine pride!"

That was all she thought it was? Controlling his temper, he took a deep breath.

"I know from experience what it is like to grow up with no father and no name," he said slowly. "To live in poverty, with a mother too distracted by her own concerns to worry about mine. She moved us to a new town every time she took a new lover. Men who inevitably despised me as a burden, who thought I deserved to be screamed at, punched, starved."

The color drained from Hallie's face.

"What?" she whispered. "She didn't protect you?"

Cristiano shook his head. "She couldn't even protect herself. When I was eighteen, her last lover beat her almost to death. When I tried to intervene, she kicked me out." He gave a hard smile. "I learned my lesson. You can only look out for yourself."

Her soft eyes looked horrified, as if she'd never imagined any family could go so wrong. "I'm so sorry."

Cristiano hated the pity in her eyes. He regretted saying so much. He'd never spoken about his past to anyone. "I just wanted you to understand." He leaned forward in his chair. "I can't let you leave with him, then spend my life wondering if you're taking good care of my son, if you've taken lovers into your house who might hate him for crying, who might pick him up out of the crib and shake him hard until the crying stops—"

"I would never let that happen!"

"I know," he said grimly. "Because he's staying with me."

"But—"

"Did you give him my last name?" he interrupted.

"His last name is Hatfield, like mine."

"Something else that our marriage will rectify," he said.

Hallie looked down at her baby softly whimpering in her arms. Her voice was small as she said with visible reluctance, "I might be willing to talk about…about shared custody."

Why was she continuing to argue? Repressing his rising anger, he shook his head. "Marriage."

"But why?"

"I've given you the reasons." Suddenly he was finished trying to reason with her, trying to explain. He'd been far more patient and open with her than she deserved. For all the good it had done. He narrowed his eyes. "The discussion is over. We will wed. The decision is made."

"Made by *you*. But you're not my boss. Not anymore."

Cristiano tilted his head. He said in a deceptively casual voice, "You can refuse my proposal, of course."

"Then I refuse."

"Then our son stays with me."

Wide-eyed, she breathed, "Just because you're his biological father you think you have the right to take him from me? I'm his mother!"

"And I have an entire team of lawyers at my disposal. What do you have? Nothing. You've already indicated you're a liar and a flight risk. I'd request an immediate injunction from a judge to prevent you from ever leaving New York."

"Liar? When did I ever lie?"

"Just now. When you took a hundred thousand dollars from me under false pretenses, then tried to run away with my son without telling me he existed."

Hallie's face was deathly pale. The baby's whimpers rose to soft wails.

"I *am* a liar," she said suddenly. "You're not Jack's father, Cristiano. You never were. It was all a…a plot. To get money from you."

"You're the worst liar I've ever seen."

"I slept with five men right after you!" Her voice rose desperately. "Any of them could be his father. Here—take your money back!"

Pulling the folded check from the pocket of her sundress, she held it out to him.

Cristiano's lips curved.

"Why, Hallie," he said, without moving to take it, "are you trying to bribe me to give up my parental rights?"

Stuffing the check back in her pocket, she rose trembling to her feet. "I wish I'd never come here!"

His voice turned hard. "Sit down."

"And I don't care what you say." She lifted her chin. "Our justice system wouldn't take a baby from his mother!"

"So dramatic." He added with dark amusement, "You have a lot of faith in something you clearly know nothing about. How do you think judges and juries decide the truth? They believe the best lawyers with the best arguments. And what kind of lawyer would you find to represent you? An inexperienced pro bono attorney fresh out of law school? Some tired hack working on contingency? You'll have no chance. You will lose."

Cristiano watched the emotions struggle on Hallie's beautiful face. Remembering how she'd almost walked out with his child, he didn't feel sorry for her. At all.

He looked down at Jack, now loudly complaining in Hallie's arms. It had been so close. It scared him to think about it. If he hadn't been suspicious and followed her into the lobby, he never would have known. His son would have grown up believing his father had abandoned him. Rejected him.

Exactly as Cristiano's father had.

Hallie looked down at her wailing baby. "He's hungry," she said, avoiding his gaze. "Where can I go?"

"Right here."

"I'm not nursing him in front of you."

"I don't trust you not to run off."

"Fine," she bit out as the baby's wails increased. "At least turn around."

"Of course." He turned toward the wall of windows overlooking the city. The baby's crying ceased almost immediately, changing to soft, contented murmurs.

Cristiano's shoulders relaxed, and he realized that he'd been tense, feeling his son's unhappiness. He felt more sure than ever that his impulsive decision, demanding marriage, was right. It was the only way to ensure the baby's comfort and security.

His son's childhood would be completely different from his own. Jack wouldn't be abandoned by a father who cared only about his business empire, or left to the devices of a mother who cared only about her own selfish needs. He would never worry about getting beaten or having enough to eat. Jack would always have a stable home. And two loving parents.

Cristiano would do whatever it took, make any sacrifice, to make it so. And so would Hallie.

He would leave her no other choice.

Rising from the white chair, still with his back to her, he pulled out his phone, pressed a button and lifted it to his ear.

"Contact Dr. Garcia," he told his executive assistant, Marcia Lattimer, when she answered. "Tell him I'm bringing a woman and baby in twenty minutes for a checkup and paternity test."

"Yes, sir."

"What?" Hallie said in alarm behind him.

"Ask Matthews to pull the limo around," he continued. He remembered the baby. "On second thought, the SUV. Have the concierge arrange a new baby seat to be sent down. Whatever is required for a three-month-old. I want it installed and ready by the time we're downstairs."

"Of course, Mr. Moretti," Marcia murmured. She was well paid to be on call around the clock. "Anything else?"

"I'll let you know," he said, and hung up.

"Paternity test?" Hallie's voice was low but enraged. "You don't even believe he's yours?"

"Can I turn around?"

"Yes."

He looked at her calmly. He was pleased to see the baby now sleeping contentedly in her arms. "You said he was mine. Then you said he wasn't."

She looked furious. "You know!"

"I believe he is mine, but I want proof."

She tossed her head. "What kind of quack doctor will do a paternity test in the middle of the night? It's after nine!"

Cristiano was amused that she thought of nine o'clock as the middle of the night. His own nights out often didn't start until eleven. "Dr. Garcia is my personal physician, one of the best in the city. He also appreciates that I fully fund his medical research."

She ground her teeth. "Is everyone in this city on your payroll? Do you always get what you want?"

"Yes," he said simply, to both.

Ten minutes later, they were seated in the back of a huge black SUV with tinted windows and a brand-new baby seat installed between them.

"Nice to meet you, ma'am," called Matthews from the driver's seat. "Cute little guy you've got there." He looked at Cristiano in the rearview mirror. "I understand congratulations are in order, sir?"

"Thank you," Cristiano said. He tenderly lifted a soft blue blanket against his sleeping baby's plump cheek. Feeling Hallie's gaze, Cristiano looked up. A current of electricity passed between them.

Biting her full, pink lower lip, she abruptly looked away. But his body was still aware of her. A new thought went through Cristiano.

He'd intended to marry her as a matter of honor and duty, but there would be compensations.

A year ago, he'd sent her away for her own good—and his. But fate had changed their lives. Now, through their child, they would always be connected.

Married.

And marriage would have other benefits. A wedding night. Endless sensual delights.

He wanted to kiss her. His gaze traced over the curve of her cheek, over the visible tremble of her pink lips as she stubbornly stared out the window into the dark city streets. He wondered how long it would take him to seduce her.

Would it be tomorrow?

Tonight?

Either way, Cristiano knew that nothing could now deny him the pleasure of taking Hallie to his bed. He would possess every inch of her. Every night. For as long as he desired.

Once they were wed, she would be his.

CHAPTER THREE

As THEY LEFT the doctor's private office downtown later that night, Hallie was in despair.

She couldn't marry him. She *couldn't*.

But how could she not?

Closing her eyes, she leaned back in the seat of the SUV and tried to picture herself as Cristiano's wife. She imagined Cristiano in a tuxedo, striding through his luxury skyscraper while she trailed after him in a dumpy maid's uniform.

How could the two of them ever marry? What did they even have in common?

Just one thing. Her gaze fell upon the baby in the car seat beside her.

What would it be like for Jack to be raised as a tycoon's son, wealthy beyond belief? To go to all the best schools, with the best tutors? To be proficient at all the sports of the wealthy, like skiing, tennis, lacrosse? Every door in the world would be open to Jack.

A lump rose in her throat. But would her son

be happy? Would he grow up to be a good, honorable man?

"Would you like me to take you home?" Cristiano said in a low voice.

Hallie looked at him over the baby seat in the back seat of the SUV. He'd taken off his tuxedo jacket and loosened his tie. His dark good looks and smoldering gaze burned through her.

"Home?" she whispered.

Cristiano lifted an eyebrow. "Whatever you might think of me, I'm not a total bastard. Now that I have proof of paternity I want you to be comfortable."

He was willing to take Hallie home? He'd given up his ridiculous plan of forcing her to marry him?

A rush of relief flooded through Hallie; it was so great she almost cried.

"Thank you," she choked out.

"Give Matthews your address."

Her address. Remembering what had happened with her landlord that morning, she gulped. She didn't want to face that horrible man again. Plus, if Cristiano saw where she'd been living, he might change his mind and refuse to let the baby live there. Hallie barely wanted to go back herself.

"Um…in the East Village," she said vaguely.

Cristiano looked at her expectantly, dark eyebrows raised. Reluctantly she gave Matthews the address.

I just won't let Cristiano go in, she told herself. The apartment building looked respectable enough on the outside. Plus, maybe her landlord was very sorry for what he'd done. Maybe.

She looked down at her baby, who'd been fed and changed at the clinic and was now happily babbling. She stroked his downy dark hair, looking into the eyes that were exactly like his father's.

Then she suddenly remembered. Reaching into her diaper bag, she grabbed her phone. Just as she'd expected, she saw multiple messages from her friends.

Are you all right? Is he being nice?

From Tess.

Did he agree to pay child support? How much?

From Lola.

Why aren't you answering?

Are you being held hostage?

Should we call the police?

Quickly Hallie typed out a response to them both.

All well. Just got a paternity test. He says he wants to be a father to Jack. More later.

She tucked her phone away. Rolling down her car window, Hallie took a deep breath, looking out into the warm, humid July night as their SUV drove into the Lower East Side. She felt sick at the thought of seeing her landlord, who wasn't a proper landlord at all, just a guy who'd been willing to rent her a room in his apartment at a cut-rate price.

But the man had made it clear to her that morning that he expected her to pay in other, less tangible ways. She gulped. She never would have wanted to come back here, except she'd left behind all her most precious possessions. Her old family photos from West Virginia. Her grandmother's homemade quilt. Her father's watch. It was everything she had left of her family now.

Hallie took a deep breath. She'd just pay the landlord off, take all her stuff and then she and the baby could check into a hotel.

"Um…" Hallie bit her lip. "Do you think we could stop somewhere so I could cash my check?"

"You waste no time." The corners of Cristiano's lips twitched. "You think some check-cashing store is going to count you out a hundred thousand dollars in twenty-dollar bills?"

"Maybe a bank…"

"The banks are closed. Why do you need money?"

"I've been having a small problem with the landlord," she said quietly. He stared at her.

"Are you under the impression that I'm leaving you and Jack at your apartment?"

She drew back, bewildered. "Aren't you?"

"We're getting your things. Jack's things. Then we're going back to my penthouse."

"Oh," she whispered.

"Put that check away. Rip it up, invest it, cash it tomorrow, whatever you want. But I'll be providing you and my son with everything you could possibly need."

His voice was autocratic. Clearly he thought he was still the boss of her. She felt shaken.

"I thought, now that you have the results of the paternity test—now that you have some legal rights—you wouldn't need to get married."

"You thought wrong." The SUV pulled up at the curb in front of the five-story building. "Get what you need for tonight. Tomorrow, I'll arrange for your lease to be paid in full. That should take care of your landlord. My staff will return to collect anything big or heavy. Cribs, furniture. Or we can leave all that behind and buy new. Whichever you prefer."

"Um," said Hallie, who owned neither a crib for the baby nor any actual furniture.

"I'll wait here with the baby and give you your privacy. Don't be long." When she didn't move, his gaze sharpened. "Well?"

Turning, she blurted, "I don't need anything. Let's just go straight to your hotel."

"But you need clothes—"

"No, I'm fine."

He looked at her as if she'd lost her mind. "But we're already here."

"I don't want to go in!" Her voice was shrill.

Cristiano looked at her for a long moment. When he spoke, his voice was surprisingly gentle.

"What's really going on, Hallie?"

With an intake of breath, she looked away. Even at midnight the street was busy, and the neon lights of pizzerias and Laundromats littering First Avenue lit up the sultry summer night.

"After you fired me," she said softly, "it was hard to find a job. I finally worked as housekeeper for a couple on the Upper West Side. The job included room and board. But when I brought Jack home from the hospital they let me go."

His eyebrows lowered. "Why?"

She gave a humorless smile. "They said Jack's crying was causing psychic trauma to their two Chinese Crested show dogs."

"Are you serious?"

"With a newborn, I couldn't find a new job. I've lived off my savings for the last three months. Even the cheapest apartments were too much." She looked down at her hands. "So last month, I rented a room in a stranger's apartment. From an online site. I was amazed it was so cheap. Then…"

She stopped, biting her lip.

Eyes narrowing, Cristiano leaned forward in the back seat.

"Then?" he demanded.

"The man wasn't bad at first. But over the last few weeks, he started brushing up against me in the kitchen. Trying to catch me coming out of the shower. That sort of thing." She looked away. It was surprisingly hard to go on. "This morning, he…grabbed me."

Silence fell in the SUV.

"He attacked you." Cristiano's voice was toneless. It gave her the courage to meet his eyes.

"Maybe *attack* is too strong a word." She tried to smile, failed. "He tried to kiss me and reach his hand under my dress. When I pushed him away, he told me I wasn't paying my fair share of the rent so I should pay in other ways." Trembling, she looked away. "I grabbed the baby and my diaper bag and ran. He yelled after me that I'd signed a lease and he'd be keeping all my things as payment. The only reason I have the stroller is because I'd left it downstairs." She whispered, "He has everything I own. But I'm not sure I can face him again."

Silence.

Slowly she looked up.

Then Hallie saw Cristiano's expression. The fire in his dark eyes. The cold fury that threatened imminent death for the man who'd scared her.

"I'm fine. Really." Putting her hands on his taut arm, she said hurriedly, "I hardly own anything. All my clothes would fit in a single duffel bag. It's just family photos and an old quilt…" She realized she was babbling and took a deep breath. "He didn't hurt me. He never threatened the baby…"

His voice was low and deadly. "He tried to force himself on you."

"I got away. Everything's fine, we're all fine—"

"*I'm* not fine," Cristiano bit out, and got out of the vehicle. He looked back at her, his handsome face as implacable as granite. "Which apartment number?"

"Promise you won't hurt him—"

"*His number,*" he ground out.

"Four C," she whispered.

His face was half-hidden in shadow in the gleam from the neon sign of a nearby bar. "Wait here."

He slammed the car door.

Hallie's wait seemed to last forever. She nervously watched the minutes pass by on the dashboard. She stroked her baby's cheek as he smiled up at her from the reverse-facing baby seat. "It's fine," she reassured Jack, who in response lifted his chubby arm to bat blindly at the giraffe toy dangling from the handle of his car seat.

Oh, she was being ridiculous. Most likely the two men were having a civilized chat, that was all. Cristiano was likely calmly writing a check—which was, after all, what he did best—

and requesting that Mervin Smith, the man who possessed the rent-controlled apartment, would kindly pack up all her things and bring them down.

Right. Not even Tess would have believed that.

Nervously she looked up at Matthews, the driver, who was still sitting at the wheel. "I don't need to worry about what Cristiano might do, right? He wouldn't do anything violent. Right?"

Matthews peered up through his window at the building. "Luther's not here. That's a good sign."

"Luther?"

"His bodyguard."

Hallie brightened. "That's true."

"But Mr. Moretti was a brawler, back when he was young. He fought his way out of the streets of Naples."

"Oh." She swallowed. "But that was a long time ago. I'm sure Cristiano has changed—"

"And just last year—" Matthews stroked his beard thoughtfully "—two punks tried to jump him as he was jogging real early through Central Park. He put them in the hospital. And then there was the time—"

"That's good," Hallie said in a strangled voice,

holding up her hand sharply. "You don't need to tell me more."

"Glad to help," the driver said, straightening his old-fashioned black cap. Then he sucked in his breath and got out of the vehicle.

Hallie jumped as her car door was suddenly wrenched open. She saw Mervin, with dried ketchup still on his chin and his too-tight T-shirt pulling up over his huge belly, on his knees on the sidewalk. He looked terrified.

"I'm sorry," he choked out. "I'm so sorry, Hallie—"

"Miss Hatfield," Cristiano corrected coldly, standing behind the man like a dark angel.

"Miss Hatfield," the man repeated desperately. "I brought down your stuff. Everything is there, totally perfect, I swear—"

"Thank you," she said anxiously. Her eyes lifted to Cristiano's. Even after what her landlord had done to her, she'd never wanted him humiliated like this. "It's all right now."

Cristiano looked down at the man with a sneer. "If I ever hear that you've attacked any woman ever again—"

"Never, ever, I swear," Mervin cried. Stumbling

to his feet, he hurried into the building with one final terrified glance back.

As Matthews stacked the few boxes into the SUV's trunk, Cristiano calmly climbed into the back seat beside her and the baby. Matthews closed the trunk with a bang. Two minutes later, they were driving north through the streets of Manhattan.

Her heart was still pounding. "What did you do to him?"

Cristiano shrugged. "I asked him to apologize."

"You just…asked?"

"I asked nicely."

She thought about pushing the issue, then decided she didn't want to know. She hadn't seen visible signs of injury. That was the best she could hope for—and that the man had been sincere when he'd said he'd never try to force a kiss on any woman again. She took a deep breath.

"Thank you," she whispered. "I don't care about the clothes. But the pictures of my family mean the world to me."

He looked at her, then set his jaw. "I'm surprised you even care about your family after they turned their backs on you."

"What do you mean?"

"They left you and Jack to struggle alone."

Hallie blinked at him in surprise, and said gently, "They didn't have a choice. They died five years ago."

Cristiano's eyes widened. "Died?"

She swallowed over the lump in her throat. It was still hard to speak of it. "Back home, in West Virginia. I grew up in a tiny village in the mountains. I was nineteen, still living at home, working the overnight shift at a grocery store in a nearby town. A fire had burned much of the forest the previous summer. After a week of hard rain, one night a flash flood came down the mountain and ripped our cabin off its foundation. If I'd been sleeping in my bed, I would have died with my parents and brother." She looked down. "For a long time, I wished I had."

"I'm sorry," he said quietly.

Blinking back tears, Hallie looked blindly out her window. "I came home at dawn and found fire trucks where my house had been. It had floated down the river, knocked to one side, crushed into wood. They found my family later…"

She couldn't go on, remembering how she'd felt at nineteen when her whole world had fallen apart, when she'd lost her home and everyone she loved without warning.

Suddenly she felt Cristiano's hand over her own.

With an intake of breath, she looked up. His eyes were black as jet.

"My mother died when I was eighteen," he said quietly. "The night she kicked me out, I decided if she still wanted her lover even after he beat her, if she cared about him more than me, then fine, I'd go. But at three in the morning, I went back. I found the house on fire."

"Arson?" Hallie breathed.

He shook his head, his lips twisting. "Nothing so deliberate. Her lover had been smoking in bed. He passed out drunk, and they both burned to death." He gave her a crooked smile. "It's funny, really. Your family died of water. Mine of fire."

"Funny," she said over the lump in her throat. All this time she'd hated Cristiano, believing him arrogant and ruthless and cold. All of which he was. But she'd never stopped to ask why.

"I'm sorry." She twined her hand in his, trying in turn to offer comfort. "You know how it feels to lose family, too. To lose a home."

For a moment, he looked at her. Then he turned,

pulling his hand away. Lights moved over them in patterns as they drove toward Midtown.

When the SUV pulled up to the grand porte co-here of the Campania Hotel, Cristiano lifted the baby's carrier from the back seat. Holding the handle with his powerful arm, he turned back to Hallie, extending his other hand to help her out of the car.

Nervously she put her hand in his. Just feeling his palm against hers as he helped her out made her shiver from her scalp to her toes.

He held her hand as they walked through the lobby with its soaring ceilings and elegant mid-century furniture. The space was filled with glam-orous people, hotel guests and patrons of the lobby bar or the jazz club. She saw a sexy sheikh, pout-ing models and starlets.

All of them turned to stare at Cristiano as he passed. Then their gazes slid in confusion to Hallie, makeup-free and wearing a limp cotton sundress. Even more shocking was the baby car-rier hanging from Cristiano's arm.

People stared and whispered as they passed. A few dared to approach Cristiano with questions in their eyes. He just nodded at them and kept walking.

He stopped only briefly to speak to Clarence Loggia, the hotel manager, as Matthews and a porter headed for the elevator with Hallie's boxes.

"Good evening, Mr. Moretti." Mr. Loggia was too well trained to show even the slightest surprise at seeing either a baby or a former hotel maid on his employer's arm.

"How is it tonight, Clarence?"

"I am pleased to report the hotel is currently at ninety-six percent capacity. The Sultan of Bataar just arrived. He's taken the presidential suite for the entire summer, along with the rest of the floor for his entourage."

"Excellent. Please send him my regards and a collection of his favorite brandy and cigars with my personal compliments."

The man smiled. "Already done, sir." He hesitated, then lowered his voice. "Also, I thought you would want to know. Prince Stefano Zacco di Gioreale just checked in."

"Why does he insist on staying here?" A shadow crossed Cristiano's face, then he shrugged. "I suppose his money is as good as any other's."

"I thought you'd say that." The manager gave an impish smile. "But in light of your past history with the gentleman, I did take the liberty of adding a surcharge to his nightly rate."

"He deserves it, the Sicilian bastard. Nicely done, Loggia. Anything else?"

"Nothing that requires your attention."

"I see I'll be leaving the hotel in good hands when I depart. *Buonasera.*"

"Good night, sir."

Cristiano turned back to her. As they walked to the elevator, suddenly Hallie felt very tired. Without a word, he stepped ahead of her to press the elevator button.

"Hallie Hatfield!"

A woman's shrill voice behind her made her jump. Turning, she saw Audrey, who'd once been her supervisor. Not just that. She'd once been a trusted mentor and friend.

"What are you doing here, Hallie?" the other woman demanded. "Looking for another rich man to seduce? You're no longer employed here and not allowed to be loitering in the lobby with the guests. Get out before I call the—"

Audrey sucked in her breath as Cristiano suddenly turned around.

"Hallie's with me," he said mildly. "And I own

the hotel, so that makes it all right, does it not, Ms...." He looked at her name tag. "Ms. Johnson?"

Audrey's shocked face went white, then red.

"Yes, of course. I'm so sorry, Mr. Moretti," she stammered, backing away. She bowed her head repeatedly. "I didn't realize Hallie was with you. I'll, um, return to my duties—"

The woman fled. As Hallie and Cristiano got into the elevator with their baby, he frowned. "That was your old supervisor."

"Yes."

"Did she always treat you so poorly?"

She gave a brief smile. "No."

"Do you want me to fire her?"

Hallie gaped at him. She couldn't tell if he was joking, but just to be safe she quickly said, "No, of course not. I feel bad for her."

"Why?"

"When you ordered her to fire me directly, without going through HR, then gave her the mysterious severance envelope she wasn't allowed to read..." Hallie shrugged. "She's not stupid. She guessed we'd slept together."

"Why would she care?"

Did he really not know? "Because she's in love with you."

"Is she?" he said carelessly. Hallie gave him a wistful smile.

"Most women are, I imagine. Even I almost was, once."

Cristiano focused abruptly on her. She felt the intensity of his gaze burn through her soul. "You were in love with me?"

She swallowed.

"For a year, I often cleaned your penthouse—did you know that?"

He shook his head.

"Anytime your regular housekeeper, Camille, was sick or needed to take her grandchildren to school." She gave a wistful smile. "Dusting your pictures, I used to look at your face and wonder what it would be like to…"

"Yes?" he said, drawing closer, putting his hand on her bare shoulder above the straps of her sundress. A hard shiver went through her.

The elevator reached their floor, and the door slid open with a ding.

"But that was before I knew you," she said steadily. "Now nothing on earth could make me love you again."

She walked out of the elevator, head held high. Cristiano reached past her to unlock the penthouse door with his fingerprint, still holding their baby's carrier on his arm.

The city skyline, sparkling through floor-to-ceiling windows, was the only light in the penthouse.

The darkness was suggestive. Intimate. Setting down the baby carrier, Cristiano turned to face her.

"I don't know about love," he said in a low voice. "It's not something I've ever felt, or wanted to feel." Reaching out, he tucked a tendril of Hallie's hair behind her ear. "But from the moment I first heard you sing, I knew you were different from any woman I'd ever known."

"Thank you." Shivering from his brief touch, she tried to smile. "That's why I came to New York. Did you know? I dreamed of becoming a world-famous singer."

For all his praise, he looked surprised. "A singer?"

Hallie gave a low laugh. "Did you think I came all the way from West Virginia because my big dream was to be a maid in your hotel?"

"No?" Cristiano smiled. "You certainly have the voice, *cara*. The heartbreak and longing of your song—you made me feel it. Your voice was the first thing I noticed about you." His eyes slid over her face, to her bare shoulders, down her curvy body beneath the cotton sundress. "Do you want to know the second thing?"

A wave of heat went through her. Her cheeks burned as she whispered, "No."

Maybe he wasn't doing it on purpose, she thought. Maybe he flirted without thinking, like breathing. He couldn't really still want her. But something in his eyes made her think—

He turned away, picking up the baby carrier. Beckoning Hallie to follow, he pushed open the first door down the hall.

"You can sleep here tonight."

Confused, she followed him into the pristine guest room that she'd cleaned many times long ago. "Who's in charge of cleaning this now?"

"Still Camille. I have no idea who her backup is." He gave her a crooked grin. "They're more careful than you were not to be seen."

With a snort, Hallie looked around the guest room. "Every time I changed these sheets, they seemed untouched. I used to wonder if the room was ever used."

He set the baby carrier gently on the floor. "It isn't."

Frowning, she turned to look at him. "Never?"

"You're my first guest."

"But surely you've invited family, friends—"

"I have no family," he said. "When friends visit, I give them their own suite downstairs."

"Oh." *No family*, she thought. And though he lived in a luxurious hotel, he had no real home. In some ways, they were the same. Strange. For a moment their eyes met. Then she saw the boxes stacked neatly in the corner. "My things!"

She rushed over and started digging through the boxes. Relief poured through her as she found the family pictures, her father's watch, her brother's old baseball trophy, her mother's music box. All the photos, still warped and faded, found on the banks of the river. Blinking away tears, she leaned back on her haunches and looked up at Cristiano.

"Everything is here. Thank you." Her voice choked. "You don't know what this means to me."

"So I'm not still an indecent excuse for a man?"

She blushed. "I never should have said—"

"It's all right." He turned away. "I'll leave you and the baby to rest."

"You're not afraid I'm going to try to run away with him in the middle of the night?"

He glanced back. "Are you planning to?"

Hallie thought of the fierce joy in Cristiano's face when he'd gotten the paternity test results that proved Jack was his son. How he'd been so protective of her. How he'd gotten her precious possessions back for her. He, too, had experienced the pain of losing family and home.

She could no longer imagine stealing Jack away when Cristiano wanted so clearly to be part of his life.

"You're Jack's father," she said in a small voice. "I wouldn't try to hurt you."

His shoulders relaxed. He motioned around the guest room and en suite bathroom. "It should be equipped with everything you require."

"And then some," she said, noticing the crib and a co-sleeper both set up on the other side of the king-size bed.

Following her gaze, Cristiano said awkwardly, "I didn't know how you and the baby prefer to sleep. My assistant said both of those were popular with new mothers."

"Thank you." She gave him a smile. "It'll be fun to use a co-sleeper that's new. The crib looks nice, too."

He gave a brief nod. "If you get hungry or need anything, just lift up the phone and dial one. It's an express line to the front desk and will be prioritized above all other calls. The staff pride themselves on answering on the first ring." Coming forward, he put his hand gently on Hallie's bare shoulder. She felt his touch race through her entire body, setting her nerves aflame.

"Until tomorrow," he said in a low voice.

After Cristiano left, closing the door behind him, Hallie took the baby carrier with her into the en suite bathroom. As Jack babbled contentedly from his carrier nearby, she took a quick, hot shower. She let all the sweat and anxiety of the long day wash off into steamy bliss. She washed her hair with the expensive shampoos and conditioners she'd once just stocked as a housekeeper. Afterward, she stepped into a soft, thick white terry-cloth robe from the heated stand. Her skin was pink and warm with steam as she came out and saw Jack was still happy in his baby carrier, cooing at the soft giraffe dangling from the handle.

"Now your turn, little one." Unbuckling him from the carrier, she cuddled him close, kissing his soft head and chubby cheeks. She gave him a warm bath in the baby bathtub she found in the bathroom cabinet along with baby shampoo. Dry-ing him off, she put him in a new diaper and clean footie pajamas.

Cuddling her baby close, she went to the soft new glider chair by the bedroom window and took a deep breath, relishing Jack's sweet, clean baby smell. After reading him a short baby book from a collection on the shelf, she fed him and rocked him to sleep, then tucked him snugly into the co-sleeper.

Hearing her stomach growl, Hallie tried to remember the last time she'd eaten. A stale cookie at the single mothers support group? It seemed a year ago. Which reminded her. She grabbed her phone from her bag and messaged Tess and Lola.

I'm staying at his penthouse tonight. He got everything back from the landlord. I think everything's going to be fine.

Plugging her cell phone in to recharge, she turned to the bulky phone plugged in to the wall. Hungry though she was, she couldn't imagine calling room service, especially so late. She'd never ordered it herself, but her parents had told her about room service after they'd gone to a hotel in Cincinnati for their twenty-fifth anniversary.

"It was so expensive!" her father had exclaimed.

"With a required twenty-percent gratuity," her mother had breathed in shock, "and a delivery fee on top of that!"

"And the food arrived cold!" he'd added indignantly. "Room service is for suckers who want to burn money!"

Hallie smiled at the memory. Her smile faded as she felt all over again how much she missed them. Then she shook her head decisively. No room service. She'd just have to find something in Cristiano's kitchen.

Tightening the belt on her white terry-cloth robe, she peeked out into the penthouse's dark hallway, telling herself that Cristiano was already asleep in his own bedroom. But when she crept into the kitchen, she saw him sitting on the white sofa in the great room, his handsome, intent face shadowed by the glow of his laptop.

Looking up, he saw her, and the smile that lit up his hard, handsome features made her heart skip a beat.

"Can't you sleep?" Closing his laptop, he rose to his feet. He must have taken a shower, because his hair was wet. His chest was bare, revealing the defined curves of his muscled torso in the moonlight streaming through the windows. He wore only low-slung drawstring pajama pants. *Very* low-slung, clinging to edges of his hips, revealing the trail of dark hair on his taut belly.

Her mouth went dry. She had to force her eyes up.

"I'm, um, hungry," she croaked, praying he couldn't read her thoughts. Licking her lips, she gazed around the room, desperate to look anywhere but at his powerful bare chest, the flat plane of his stomach or the drawstring pants barely clinging to his hips.

"Did you call room service?"

What did room service have to do with anything? Oh, yes. She'd said she was hungry. Her eyes met his, and he gave her a sensual, heavy-lidded smile. She blushed to realize that he had caught her looking after all.

"It's not necessary. I'll just rummage in your fridge if that's all right."

Cristiano looked amused. "Go right ahead."

But as she opened the door of his sleek, commercial-grade refrigerator, she was disappointed to see only an expensive bottle of vodka and some martini olives.

She turned back with a frown. "Where is your food?"

"I don't cook."

Peeking in his freezer, she saw ice cubes. That was it. No ice cream or even frozen broccoli past its sell-by date.

She'd known from her time cleaning the penthouse that Cristiano Moretti wasn't exactly a chef, but the level of emptiness shocked her. Hallie looked through the cupboards with increasing desperation. They were empty except for a few items that belonged in a wet bar. Disappointed, she looked at him accusingly.

"Don't you even snack?"

He shrugged. "I lead a busy life. Why own a hotel if I don't use the amenities?"

"No one can hate cooking this much."

He gave her a sudden grin. "I prefer to think of it as quality assurance. What can I say? I'm a workaholic."

"I know," she sighed.

"Get room service."

She shook her head. "It's the middle of the night. And do you know how much it costs?"

He looked amused again. "You do know I own this hotel?"

She tried not to stare at the curve of his sensual lips. Then she realized she'd just licked her own. Her blush deepened. She croaked, "That's no excuse to—"

"I'll order it for you." He went to the kitchen phone on the marble counter. Picking it up, he looked at her in the shadowy kitchen. "What do you want?"

Want? What a suggestive question. Hallie's gaze lingered on his broad shoulders, his powerful arms, his muscular chest dusted with dark hair. She could see the outline of his powerful thighs beneath the thin knit fabric of his drawstring pants. He gave her a wicked smile. She realized he'd caught her looking again.

Quick, say something intelligent to distract him! she told herself desperately.

"Um…what do you recommend?"

No!

His eyes gleamed. "Shall I tell you?"

Her heart was pounding in her throat. "I'll have a cheeseburger and fries," she said quickly. "And a strawberry shake."

Cristiano's sensual lips curved, as if he knew exactly how her blood was racing and her heart was pounding. She was suddenly afraid to even meet his gaze. Turning to the phone, he gave the order swiftly, then hung up. "Your dinner will be here in nine minutes."

Hallie looked at him incredulously. "Nine minutes? That's impossible."

"Know all about room service, do you?" He sounded amused again.

"My parents told me horror stories. Cold food, small portions, no ketchup, then a big bill."

"Let's test out your theory." He lifted an eyebrow. "Care to place a friendly wager?"

"What kind of wager?"

Going back to the sofa, he sat down and patted the cushion beside him.

She sat down hesitantly beside him, perching awkwardly on the edge of the sofa. She was suddenly aware that she was naked beneath her bathrobe. Nervously she pulled it a little tighter around her. "What do you have in mind?"

"If your food arrives within—" he glanced at his platinum watch "—seven minutes and forty-eight seconds, I win. If it doesn't, you win."

"What do I win?"

His eyes flickered. "What if I cook breakfast for you tomorrow?"

She snorted. "Cereal?"

Cristiano shook his head. "Eggs and bacon. Belgian waffles. Anything you want."

She was impressed in spite of herself. "But you hate cooking."

"I won't have to do cook."

"You won't?"

"Because I'm not going to lose."

The man had confidence, she'd give him that. "And if you do win, what would you want from me?"

His dark eyes glinted wickedly.

"A kiss."

A rush of need crackled through her body as her lips tingled in anticipation. She croaked, "What?"

"You heard me."

She couldn't risk placing this bet. She hated him. Didn't she? Not exactly. Not anymore. But she definitely didn't want him to kiss her. Did she? Okay, maybe she did, but she knew it would lead to disaster. On that, her body and brain and heart agreed. *She could not let him kiss her again.*

Yet Hallie was unable to look away from his hungry gaze. "Why would you want to kiss me?"

"Why not?" he said lazily.

Was he bored? Or just suggesting it to throw

her off-kilter and make clear his power over her? "No, thanks. I'm not the gambling kind."

"I think you are. If you refuse my wager, then you're admitting that you might be wrong." He leaned toward her on the white sofa, almost close enough to touch. "And I might be right."

Her heart was in her throat. "About room service?"

"About everything," he whispered, his lips almost grazing her cheek.

She shivered at his closeness. Then she realized what he was saying and that he was talking about far more important issues than food.

"I admit no such thing." Still, as she drew back sharply, his gaze fell to her knee, and she realized that her robe had slipped open to reveal her crossed leg all the way to her thigh. Cheeks aflame, she covered her legs.

His eyebrow lifted. "Then take the bet."

"Fine," she snapped. "I'll enjoy watching you cook for me tomorrow." She lifted her chin. "But in addition to the food being delivered on time, to prove me wrong it also has to be the best cheeseburger, fries and shake I've ever had."

"It will be," he said without hesitation, and held out his hand. She stared at it for a moment, then shook it as quickly as she could, desperately ignoring her body's reaction at that brief touch.

And so it was that exactly five minutes and four seconds later, a full fifteen seconds before the deadline, she found herself looking despondently at the white linen-covered room-service tray resting on the coffee table. As Cristiano got up to chat with the smiling room-service waiter, she sighed. Even the incredible smell of hot French fries wafting through the air could offer no comfort. She knew she was about to lose their bet.

A kiss.

Hallie put her hands on her forehead. Why had she ever agreed to it? *Why?* How could she have been so stupid? Cristiano got room service all the time! He knew how long it took! He knew how good the food was!

Did she *want* him to kiss her?

But that was a question Hallie didn't want to answer, not even to herself, as the waiter left and Cristiano came back. Turning on a lamp, he looked down at her. His cruel, sensual lips curved. "Don't look so frightened."

She lied. "I'm not."

"You're terrified." Lifting the silver lid off the

tray, he said idly, "Do you think I intend to take my kiss now, and ravish you against the wall?"

With a flash of heat, images came to her mind. Mouth dry, she croaked, "I—"

"Why don't you try it?" he murmured, sitting beside her on the sofa. "See if you like it?"

Her heart nearly stopped. She looked at him, lips parted.

He held out a French fry.

"Decide," he said huskily, "if it's the best you've ever had."

She stared from the French fry to the challenge in his eyes. Snatching the fried potato from his fingers, she licked off the salt, then popped the whole length into her mouth. It was so hot, salty and delicious that she gave an involuntary groan of pleasure.

"So…good…" she breathed, briefly lost in ecstasy.

A strangled noise came from the back of his throat. Looking up, she saw his handsome face looked strained.

Clearing his throat, he rose from the sofa. "I'll leave you to enjoy it."

"Wait. I haven't tried the rest." Although she knew, even before she picked up the cheeseburger, that it would be the best she'd ever had. She took a big bite, licking a splash of ketchup and mustard off her lips, then washed it all down with a milkshake of fresh strawberries whirled into vanilla ice cream. The milkshake was so thick she had to suck hard on the straw.

Finally she looked up, defeated. "All right, you win—"

Her voice cut off when she saw his face. He looked hungry, ruthless. Something in his eyes was dark and wild. He took a step toward her, his hands gripped at his sides, and the memory of his words flashed in her mind.

Do you think I intend to ravish you against the wall?

She shrank back from the fire in his eyes. "No."

That one word, whispered soft as a breath, seemed tangible in the air, like a wall between them. He blinked. His expression changed as if a shutter had gone down. His civilized mask slid back into place.

"Good night," he said hoarsely. Turning, he hurried down the hall toward the master bedroom.

Hallie sat alone on the sofa, shivering from what had just happened. Except nothing had happened, she told herself, struggling to calm her breath. Nothing at all.

After turning off the lamp, she stared out blankly at the lights of the moonlit city. Woodenly she ate the rest of her meal. All she could think about was how badly she'd wanted him in that moment. But the word that had escaped from her lips was *no*. Because she was afraid.

Before her night with Cristiano, Hallie had barely been kissed. She'd had a few awkward kisses with her boyfriend in high school, who'd never tried to press the issue—with good reason, as it turned out, because as soon as he left for university he announced on Facebook that he was gay. And one time, Joe Larson, the mine owner's son, had tried to force his tongue down her throat at a company Christmas party. Before Cristiano, that had been the sum total of her sexual experience.

And now he wanted to kiss her?

Now he wanted to *marry* her?

She was way out of her league.

Rising from the sofa, she walked heavily back to the guest room, where she found Jack sleeping peacefully. Putting on underwear and pajamas, she brushed her teeth and crawled into the bed next to her baby, knowing she wouldn't sleep a wink.

But, somehow, she did. She rose only once in the night, to feed the baby. When Jack next woke her with a hungry whimper, she saw golden light flooding the window. She sat up in shock, realizing that she'd just had the best night's sleep in months. How was that possible?

"Good morning, sweetheart," she said, smiling at the baby, who gurgled and waved his arms at her.

When mother and baby came out into the main room some time later, both of them were dressed—Hallie in a soft pink sundress of eyelet cotton and sandals, the baby in a onesie and blue knit shorts. She stopped when she saw Cristiano sitting at the kitchen counter. Her cheeks went hot at the memory of last night. *But why?* she said to herself. Nothing had happened!

"Good morning." Cristiano's voice was gravelly as he set down his newspaper. "I trust you slept well?"

Hallie shifted her baby's weight on her hip as she stood uncertainly in the kitchen, beneath a shaft of golden light from the windows. His eyebrows lifted as he waited. His handsome face was courteous, his dark eyes civilized. Nothing like he'd looked last night…

She shivered.

"Hallie?"

She jumped. "I slept well. Thank you."

Hallie wondered when he would kiss her. She felt the weight of that debt between them. *It's just a kiss*, she told herself, but she couldn't quite believe it. She tried to tell herself that now that he'd had time to recover from the shock of learning he was a father, Cristiano probably wouldn't repeat his demand for marriage. But looking into his hard-edged face, she couldn't believe that, either. Cristiano Moretti was the kind of man who would stop at nothing to get what he wanted.

He wanted to secure possession of their child. She knew that. But now she knew he wanted more.

He wanted her.

Nodding toward the marble countertop and holding out a china cup edged with fourteen-karat gold, he said gruffly, "Have a seat."

"Thanks." Sitting down on one of the high barstools, keeping her baby securely in her lap, she watched in surprise as he poured her a cup of steaming hot coffee from a silver carafe. "You made coffee?"

"Room service." He nodded at the tray. "There's cream and sugar."

"Thanks." Too late, she saw the wheeled carts nearby and felt foolish. Adding copious amounts of cream and sugar to her coffee, she took a sip and sighed with pleasure. Glancing at him, she said shyly, "Would you like to hold the baby?"

Cristiano hesitated, looking down at the plump, babbling three-month-old. He shook his head. "Maybe later."

"All right." She was surprised anyone could resist holding Jack, with his adorably goofy smile and his fat little cheeks.

"I ordered you a breakfast tray. It's been here an hour, so it might be cold." Cristiano turned back to his newspaper.

"Thanks." She didn't feel hungry at all. She gave him a sideways glance. "You're reading in Italian."

He didn't look up. "Yes."

"And on paper rather than on a tablet."

"So?"

"It's very retro," she ventured.

He didn't answer. He seemed barely aware of her, while her hands were shaking from being this close to him. Had she somehow imagined the way he'd looked at her last night? Had he already forgotten that he'd demanded a kiss—and marriage?

Sitting at the marble counter that separated the sleek kitchen from the great room, Hallie looked slowly around his penthouse. Modern art was splashed across the walls. Strange, heavy sculptures were displayed on columns. Once Jack started to pull himself up and walk, those would be dangerous.

But such unimaginable luxury and style. So different from how she'd grown up. A flash of memory came to her of the cabin in the West Virginia hills, with its worn wood exterior, sagging furniture and peeling linoleum.

But so comfortable for all that. So full of love. Her beloved home. Her parents. Her older brother.

Gone. All gone.

They would never know her son.

A sudden pain, like a razor blade in her throat, made her gasp as fresh, unexpected grief ambushed her.

Setting down his newspaper, Cristiano looked at her sharply. "What is it?"

Blinking fast, she looked at him. She swallowed. "I was just remembering…"

"What?"

Jack fussed a little in her arms. She was grateful for the excuse to turn away. "Nothing."

Getting up, she set the baby down in his new play gym with a padded blanket on the floor, so he could bat at the brightly colored mobile overhead. She felt Cristiano's gaze on her as she went to the room-service carts and lifted a silver lid. Taking the plate of food and silverware, she returned to sit beside him at the counter. She forced herself to take a bite, then another. The waffles and bacon were indeed lukewarm, and all she could feel was sad.

"Can I ask you something?" Cristiano asked, setting his fork down on his own empty plate.

"What?"

"Why did you refuse my marriage proposal yesterday?"

She glanced at him. "I told you—"

"That we hate each other. I remember." He took a drink of black coffee. The dainty china cup looked incongruous in his large, masculine hands. "It's just funny. I always thought if I ever asked a woman to marry me, the reaction would be very different."

"But you didn't ask. You told." Hallie looked

at her limp waffles. "And I'm not convinced you know what commitment means."

"How can you say that?"

Setting down her fork, Hallie stared out at the view of the city and bright blue skies. "My parents married straight out of high school. They fought all the time, but never threatened to leave. We were a family. And family means sticking together, no matter what." Her voice choked, and she looked down at the marble floor. "After they died, it was all I dreamed about. Having a family again. A home."

"That's why you were still a virgin when we met," he said slowly. "You were waiting for the man you could give your life to. Not just your life. Your loyalty."

She nodded, unable to meet his eyes, bracing herself for his cynical, mocking response.

Instead, his voice was quiet. "I destroyed all your plans by seducing you."

Hallie's gaze lifted to his. Then she looked at their baby in his play gym. Jack was stretching out his chubby arms, waving them like a drunken sailor as he tried to reach the mobile hanging over his head. With a trembling smile, she shook her head.

"How can I blame you, when that night brought our baby? Besides." She stared down at her hands. "What happened wasn't just your fault. It was also mine." With a deep breath, she said, "If I had really wanted to wait for marriage, I wouldn't have let you or anyone else change my mind. No matter how badly I wanted you. Because I knew even then that I could never be more than a one-night stand to a man like you."

"You're wrong." His voice was low. "You were always more than a one-night stand to me."

"So that's why you had me fired and tossed out of the hotel?" Her lips lifted humorously. "Because you wanted to spend more time with me?"

"You were an employee. A virgin. But from the moment I first heard you sing, from the moment I saw you, floating my sheets softly through the air, I had to have you. I smashed every rule."

"You knew I was a virgin?" she breathed.

He gave a slow nod. "I could tell when I kissed you. But I still couldn't stop myself from taking you to my bed. And once I had you," he said softly, "I only wanted more."

"Then why did you send me away?" she said, trembling.

His eyes met hers evenly. "I was afraid you'd

want a relationship. That you'd ask for a commitment."

His words burned her pride. "But I didn't."

"No," Cristiano agreed. He leaned toward her at the counter. "But now I'm asking you. I want us to give our son a home. To be a family." Leaning forward, he took both her hands in his own, his eyes intense. "I'm asking you to marry me."

She sucked in her breath as all her childhood dreams clamored around her. Could it truly happen? Could a night of passion turn them unexpectedly into a family?

A home.

Loyalty.

Family.

He was offering her everything she'd ever wanted, and unimaginable wealth and luxury, too.

For a moment, Hallie was tempted. Then she shook her head slowly.

"Why?" he demanded.

She turned away from his arrogant gaze, busying herself with tackling a thick, salty slice of bacon. "A marriage of convenience? How would that even work?"

"I never said it would be a marriage of convenience." His black eyes pierced hers. "Our marriage would be very real, Hallie."

Beneath his gaze, she felt hot all over. She swallowed the bacon, barely tasting it. Her full breasts were suddenly heavy, her nipples aching and taut. Tension coiled, low and deep, in her belly.

Swallowing, she pushed the plate away. "You could have any woman for the asking." She looked at Cristiano's elegant penthouse, and the wide windows that showed all New York City at his feet. "Why not wait for someone you love? Someone—" her voice faltered "—who loves you?"

"I'm thirty-five years old, and I've never loved anyone. I never thought I had the ability." Cristiano looked at Jack, wriggling happily on the soft quilted mat of the baby gym. "Until the day I found out I had a son."

Hallie felt her heart constrict as she saw the way he looked at Jack. In their intense love for their child, they were the same.

He turned back to her. "And now I know this. My duty is to protect you both. To provide for you. To give you a home. To give you my name. I offer you my loyalty, Hallie. For a lifetime."

"Your loyalty," she whispered.

Cristiano looked at her, his eyes black as night. "I will protect our son. No matter the cost."

His words sounded strangely like a warning. But that didn't make sense. Why would he warn Hallie that he intended to protect their son?

So much she'd thought about him was all wrong. He actually wanted to commit to her. To be a father to Jack.

Her son would have financial security, the best schools, the promise of a brilliant future.

And, even more importantly, Cristiano would always protect him and watch his back. If anything ever happened to Hallie, Jack would still be safe. She'd learned the hard way about loss.

Cristiano was offering her everything and, still, some part of her hesitated. "You're asking me to give up love—all hope of it forever."

"Have you ever been in love?"

"No," she was forced to admit.

"Then how can you miss what you've never had?"

His words were starting to make the impossible seem reasonable. "A marriage implies faithfulness..."

"Which I would be."

Her breath caught in her throat. She hadn't expected that. Cristiano Moretti, the famous billionaire playboy, was promising total fidelity. To her.

That thought was too outlandish to believe. She shook her head, her lips curving up at the edges. "Have you really thought this through? No more Russian supermodels?"

"You persist in underestimating me," he said softly. Reaching out, he tucked hair behind her ear. "When will you learn the truth?"

Hallie swallowed. "What's that?"

His gaze cut through her. "I want only you."

Her heart was pounding. A year ago, when he'd tossed her to the curb, she'd thought she'd made the worst mistake of her life. For the last year, she'd barely held on sometimes, trying to keep a roof over her baby's head. Security had seemed like a fairy tale.

Now Cristiano was offering her everything she'd dreamed of. She could secure her son's comfort and give him two parents and a stable home for a lifetime.

The only cost would be her heart. Their marriage would be about partnership and, yes, passion. But not love.

Could she accept that? For the rest of her life?

Or would her heart shrivel up and die?

Getting up from the barstool, Hallie crossed the great room uncertainly. She looked down at her sweet baby, cooing and playing happily. Holding her breath, she stared out the windows at the gray city and brilliant blue sky.

Silence fell in the penthouse. She felt the warm morning sun against her skin, the rise and fall of her own breath. Then she heard him cross the floor. Putting his hands on her shaking shoulders, he turned her to face him. His dark eyes burned like fire.

"One more thing," he said in a low voice. "Before you decide."

And pulling her roughly against his body, he lowered his mouth to kiss her.

CHAPTER FOUR

HIS LIPS WERE hot and yearning, burning through Hallie's body and soul. This kiss was different from the hungry, demanding passion of their first night. This time he tempted rather than took. He lured rather than ravished.

His hands tangled in her dark hair, stroking slowly down her bare shoulders and back. Shivers of need cascaded through Hallie's body. She could not resist his embrace, as wistful and tender as his whispered words, which still hung between them like mist.

When will you learn the truth?

What's that?

I want only you.

Her mind scattered in a million different directions, the penthouse whirling around her. She felt his desire for her through his low-slung pajama pants. She gripped his naked, powerful shoulders, feeling that Cristiano was the only solid thing in a world spinning out of control. His skin felt warm, his body solid and strong. This kiss, the sweet dream of his lips on hers, was all that felt real.

He deepened the embrace, pushing her back against the white sofa, his hands running over her body—over her naked arms, the spaghetti straps of her sundress. As the kiss intensified, hunger built between them until she kissed him back desperately, her whole body on fire. She gripped his shoulders, his mouth hot and demanding against hers. Feeling the sweet weight of his body over hers, the hard warmth of his muscular chest, she would have done anything—agreed to anything— to make this moment last...

"Say you'll marry me," he whispered against her skin. "Say it—"

"Yes," she choked out. She didn't realize she'd spoken until he pulled back, searching her gaze.

"You won't take it back? You won't change your mind?"

She shook her head. "It's what I want most. Loyalty. Family. Home."

"And this." And Cristiano kissed her, consuming her, until all that was left of her was fire and ash.

Cristiano had to take her to bed. Now.

If he didn't have her, now that he knew she was going to be his wife, he thought he might explode.

"You've made me so happy, *cara mia*," he whispered, kissing her forehead, her cheeks. The sweet intoxication of her lips. He started to lift her in his arms, intending to seal the deal immediately in his bedroom.

Then his baby son gave a low whimper.

"Jack," Hallie said immediately, and the sensual spell was broken. Looking at each other, they both gave a rueful laugh. Moving back, he let her get off the sofa.

After hurrying across the room, she scooped Jack up from his play gym. The baby immediately brightened in his mother's arms. "But I'm being greedy." Walking with him back to where Cristiano stood, she gave him a shy smile. "Do you want to hold him?"

He shook his head. To be honest, the baby seemed happier with his mother. And he couldn't blame Jack for preferring her. What experience did Cristiano have with children? He couldn't bear the thought of his son crying. What if he held him wrong again and Hallie scorned him for being a clumsy fool?

"Are you sure?" Hallie said, looking disappointed. But she didn't wait for an answer. She just smiled down at her son, crooning, "How are you, sweet boy?"

Cristiano's heart expanded as he looked at them, his tiny baby son with the chubby cheeks, held by his incredibly loving, sexy bride-to-be. Reaching out, he put his hand on his son's soft, downy hair. His eyes locked with Hallie's and he felt a current of emotion.

It was too much. Feeling his heart in his throat, he abruptly turned away. "We've been stuck in this penthouse long enough. I want to buy you an engagement ring."

"It's not necessary."

"But it is." He'd buy her the most obscenely huge diamond that the world had ever seen. "And our wedding must be arranged quickly, before I leave for Italy."

"You're going to Italy?"

"Tomorrow night."

"So soon!"

He turned to her with a frown. "I will visit my hotel in Rome. Also I'm building a new hotel on the Amalfi Coast and want to supervise the final preparations before the grand opening next month."

"How long will you be gone?"

"It doesn't matter, because you're both coming with me."

Hallie's eyes became round as saucers. "You want to take me and Jack to Italy?"

"Is that a problem?"

"I don't have a passport."

"Something we'll fix today, after we go to the jewelry store—and get our wedding license."

"You want us to be married in Italy?"

"That would take too long. The laws there are complicated."

Her lips parted. "You want us to be married before we leave?"

"Yes," he said roughly.

"A wedding? In *two days*?"

"Tomorrow," he said.

Hallie looked shocked. Coming forward, he took her in his arms and kissed her. "Everything will be perfect," he whispered, cupping her cheek. "I swear to you."

"All right." Looking dazed, she gave him a crooked smile. "I'll take your word for it. After all, you were right about the room service."

He returned her grin. "I'll go get dressed." His body protested at the thought of putting on clothes instead of taking Hallie's clothes *off*. Still, he could wait the few hours until they were alone, until they weren't being watched so keenly by their three-month-old chaperone. Glancing down at his pajama pants, he turned toward his bedroom, intending to find a shirt and trousers. "We'll leave in five minutes."

Behind him, Hallie gave a laugh that came straight from her belly, deeper and more heartfelt than he'd ever heard from her before. "Oh, we will, will we?"

Frowning, he turned back.

"What's so funny?" he said suspiciously.

"Nothing." She gave him a grin. "Except you're used to people always being ready whenever you want them to be, aren't you?"

"I'm a busy man. Others wait for me. I don't wait for them."

"Not anymore." She giggled. "Now you have a baby."

She was right. It was, in fact, over an hour before they left the penthouse. In that time, the baby was fed, then he'd cried, and then they had to change his clothes when he spit up all over his onesie. He was burped a little more and cried some more. Then the real reason for Jack's earlier fussiness was revealed—a blowout needing a diaper change and yet another new outfit. Hallie calmly repacked everything in her diaper bag. Finally, just as they were about to leave, the baby let out a whimper and needed to be fed again.

Through it all, Cristiano was impressed with Hallie's infinite patience and skill. He wouldn't have had a clue what to do. When she'd looked up at him with a gentle smile and asked if he wanted to help burp or change the baby, he had been filled with alarm. He'd shaken his head. What did he know? Better to leave it to the expert. Patient and loving, Hallie was clearly born to be a mother.

Once again Cristiano congratulated himself on securing his possession of her.

By the time they were out of the hotel and on the street, he took a big breath of fresh air. Yellow taxi cabs raced down the avenue as backpack-carrying tourists fought for space on the sidewalk with lawyers in suits and food carts selling everything from hot dogs to cupcakes to falafel. The summer morning was warm and fresh, and the sunlight spilled gold on the streets of New York.

But the brightest glow of all came from Hallie's sparkling eyes as she snapped their baby's carrier into his expensive new stroller.

"Thank you for this, by the way," she said, nodding at the stroller.

He'd told Marcia to send the best one. "Does Jack like it?"

She turned it toward him. "See for yourself."

Peeking down, he saw that his baby, who'd spent the past hour causing a fuss, was nestled in the stroller cozily, smiling.

Cristiano's heart swelled in his chest as his son stretched up his chubby little hands, as if reaching for the towering hotel.

"All yours someday," he told Jack softly in Italian. Then he looked at Hallie's beautiful face as she pointed up at the top of the hotel in the clouds, talking tenderly to their son. Under his breath in the same language, he added, "All mine."

Hallie turned to him quizzically. "Did you say something?"

"Just that our first stop this morning is to get our marriage license." As they waited briefly outside the hotel, he took her hand. He felt it tremble at the intimacy of the gesture.

The black SUV with tinted windows pulled up. Matthews was at the wheel and Luther, the bodyguard, sat beside him in the front.

As Matthews folded the stroller into the trunk, Cristiano opened the door for Hallie. He snapped the baby carrier securely in the back seat, then followed her inside.

"Where to, sir?" Matthews said cheerfully as Hallie smiled down at the chattering baby.

"The city clerk's office downtown."

An hour later, they left with their marriage license. Cristiano exhaled deeply. *One step closer.* In twenty-four hours it would be permanent. He would give Jack his last name. And not just the baby…

His eyes lingered on Hallie as she climbed back into the waiting SUV, tucking their smiley baby into his car seat.

He could hardly wait to possess her in bed. Tonight. This afternoon. He paused. Or he could wait to make love until their wedding night, as Hallie had once wanted.

Could he give her that? Could he wait until she was legally his to bed her? Knowing that, after tomorrow, she would be his forever?

No. He couldn't.

"Now where, sir?"

Leaning forward in the SUV, Cristiano named the most exclusive jewelry store on Fifth Avenue. He glanced at Hallie to see if it met with her approval, but she was busy playing peekaboo with the baby.

When they arrived, Hallie stared out of the window, wide-eyed at the sight of the luxury jewelry store. "Here?"

"Here," he said firmly. He intended to woo her. Perhaps he couldn't do love, but he knew about romance. Though he'd never shopped for an engagement ring before.

As Cristiano got out, he saw Hallie unbuckling their baby from the car seat. "You're bringing him with us?" he asked in surprise.

"Of course I am." As Matthews got the stroller from the back, she smiled down at her baby, tucking him inside it. "What would you expect me to do, leave him alone in the car?"

"He wouldn't be alone," Cristiano said, nonplussed. He'd intended to romance her, and even with his limited experience of babies, he'd already seen that they could be a distraction from romance. He'd told Luther to remain in the SUV, as bodyguards also could impinge on intimate moments. "Matthews and Luther could watch him."

She glanced back at the two burly men, and her lips curved. "Not exactly trained baby professionals. No offense."

"None taken, ma'am," Matthews said.

"None whatsoever," Luther said.

"Va bene." Cristiano gave in with grace. Perhaps Hallie was right, anyway. The engagement ring wasn't meant to cement just the two of them as a couple, but the three of them as a family. Still, he made a mental note that they should acquire a—what had she called it?—a *trained baby professional* as soon as possible. Because he had sensual plans for Hallie, and he knew she wouldn't be able to linger in his bed unless she was certain Jack was being well tended.

"We won't be here long," he said, as they pushed the stroller past the doorman and security guard into the gilded jewelry store. Smiling down at Hallie, he said huskily, "I already know what I want."

"I think you've made that clear," she said, her cheeks a charming shade of pink. So were her lips.

Cristiano stopped abruptly inside the entrance, beneath the stained-glass cupola high overhead. Not caring who might see, he pulled Hallie into his arms, her pink sundress fluttering behind her.

Ruthlessly he lowered his mouth to hers, kissing her long and lingeringly. The stained-glass cupola dappled them with colored light. He heard whispers and romantic sighs as some customers walked by, as well as the irritated grumbling of men as their partners hissed, "Why do you never kiss me in public like that?"

When Cristiano finally pulled away, he looked down, relishing the dazzled look in Hallie's brown eyes. Gently he traced her swollen bottom lip with his thumb.

"Soon," he whispered. "Very soon."

Hallie sucked in her breath as if still in a trance. Taking a step, she nearly stumbled. He felt a surge of supremely masculine satisfaction.

"Let me help." With a wicked grin, he took the stroller with one arm and her hand with the other. "Let's have some fun."

He already knew exactly the ring he wanted: the biggest diamond in the store. Maybe Hallie didn't care about luxuries like room service, but every woman wanted an amazing engagement ring. And Hallie would have the best.

The store manager's face lit up upon seeing Cristiano, who, though he'd never bought a ring, had purchased expensive bracelets and necklaces for various mistresses in the past. The man took them swiftly to a private room, where he spread out a selection of diamond engagement rings across a black velvet tray.

"Which would the lady like to see first?" purred the manager, who was short and sophisticated in a designer suit.

"Which is the best?" Cristiano said.

With an approving smile, the manager pointed at a middle ring, an enormous emerald-cut canary diamond set in platinum. Cristiano nodded. "That's the one."

He was surprised to see Hallie frown, her eyebrows furrowed. "But it's yellow."

"A special type of diamond, very rare and beautiful," the manager intoned, "for a rare and beautiful woman."

Staring at him, Hallie burst into a laugh. "And here I was thinking that since the color's off, we might get a discount."

The manager's smile froze in place. "It's the most luxurious diamond we possess, with a cost that is, of course, commensurate with its rare beauty."

"Try it on," Cristiano said.

Biting her lip, Hallie allowed him to slide it over her finger. Her eyes were huge as she stared down at the ring. The rectangular yellow diamond was so huge it extended over her ring finger to partially cover the two adjacent fingers.

"Twenty and a half carats," said the manager reverently.

Her hand shook visibly, and she yanked it off suddenly and placed it back on the black velvet tray.

"You don't like it?" Cristiano asked, confused.

Hallie shook her head. "It weighs like a billion pounds! It's cold! And the setting scratched my skin. What if I scratched the baby?"

"Hurt the baby?" he said incredulously. Any other woman he'd known would have grabbed the million-dollar ring with a fervent *thank you*.

Hallie shook her head. "I wouldn't want to worry about gouging out someone's eye with that thing." She tilted her head. "And since we're getting married tomorrow, why do we even need an engagement ring? It seems silly."

There was a suppressed scream from the other side of the counter. The manager looked as if he might have the vapors.

Cristiano turned back to her with a frown. "You don't want a ring?"

She put her hand in his.

"I'd rather just get a plain gold wedding band. For each of us."

Now he was really confused. "Doesn't a diamond symbolize forever? Exactly as you wanted?"

"It does," agreed the manager, nodding vigorously.

"Not for me." She entwined her smaller hand in his. "My parents just had gold bands. I don't need a big diamond or a big wedding. It's the commitment I care about. Knowing the baby's safe. That I am, too."

Her big, brown eyes were like pools to drown in. Cristiano could not argue with her. He turned to the manager.

"You heard the lady. Get her what she wants."

The manager's face fell at seeing his easy million-dollar sale slip through his fingers. Then he seemed to recall that a man such as Cristiano would be likely to buy other expensive trinkets for his wife over time, and he recovered.

"I know just the thing," the man said.

Ten minutes later, Cristiano walked out of the jewelry store into the sunshine with his beautiful bride-to-be pushing the stroller. From her wrist dangled a small red bag, which held two simple wedding bands in shining gold.

Calling an enormous diamond ring silly? Cristiano shook his head with wonder. Truly, Hallie was one in a million. But, seeing her smile, he was glad he'd let her have her way.

He had another surprise for her, too.

"Now we need to get you some clothes," he said after the SUV picked them up. He hid a smile. The surprise had taken some effort to arrange.

"Why?" Hallie looked puzzled. She looked down at her faded pink sundress and her slightly scuffed sandals. "What's wrong with this?"

"You'll need a wedding dress. We'll get the rest of your trousseau in Rome."

She gave a laugh. *"Trousseau?"*

Her expression made him feel old-fashioned, or at least *old*. "That is the word, is it not, for the traditional new wardrobe for a bride?"

Her grin widened. "That's the dumbest thing I ever heard. Why would I need new clothes to be a wife?"

"Because you're going to be *my* wife. There will be certain expectations."

"What expectations?"

She was blushing, as if she assumed he was speaking of sex. But he would hardly talk dirty with his driver, his bodyguard and their innocent baby all listening in. His lips quirked. "I am the owner of twenty-two luxury hotels around the world. That makes me the advocate for my brand. As my wife, you will be, as well."

"So?"

"So you need new clothes."

"You mean sexy? Expensive?"

"Sleek. Cosmopolitan." He ran his fingertips slowly down the side of her dress. The cotton fabric was rough and pilled from repeated washings. "I can't have my wife's clothes looking like they were bought at a discount shop. What would my shareholders think?"

"That I'm good with money and know how to get good value?" she replied archly.

He snorted. "In private, of course, you can wear whatever you want. I like the look of you in everything." Leaning forward, he whispered for her ears alone, "Or nothing."

He felt her shiver, felt his own body rise. He had to fight the urge to grab her and kiss her again. *Soon*, he promised himself hungrily. *Tonight.*

Cristiano leaned back against the SUV's soft leather seat. "You will need clothes that you can wear to events where you will be photographed and appear in newspapers as a symbol of the Campania brand."

"I didn't sign up for that."

"And yet it is so." He tilted his head curiously. "Most women would not object so strenuously to a new wardrobe."

"I'm remembering something I read in high school…that you should beware any relationship that requires new clothes."

His lips lifted. "You're talking about Thoreau. He didn't say beware the new relationship, he said beware the new enterprise."

"Marrying you, it doesn't sound like there's a difference," she said grumpily. The SUV stopped, and she frowned. "What are we—"

Then Hallie turned, and her jaw dropped when she saw Cristiano's surprise.

CHAPTER FIVE

HALLIE STOOD IN front of a full-length mirror, turning to look at herself from all angles. This wedding dress was deceptively simple, made of duchess satin with a bias cut. It made her post-pregnancy figure look amazing in a way that even she couldn't deny.

"That's it!" Lola yelled. "That's the one!"

"It's perfect," Tess said dreamily. "You look like a princess."

Hallie had been shocked to see Lola and Tess waiting for her on the curb in front of the luxury bridal shop on Fifth Avenue. Amazed, she'd stared back at Cristiano in shock. "What did you... How did you?"

He'd given her a wicked smile. "Your friends called the front desk of the hotel this morning, demanding to know if I'd kidnapped you, since you weren't responding to their messages."

"Oh," she'd said sheepishly. She had turned

off her phone last night and forgotten to turn it back on.

"I told them to come see you for themselves. They're going to help you pick out a wedding dress. If you want."

"Are you serious?"

His smile widened. "Then you all have appointments for spa treatments next door."

She'd beamed at him, then her joy had faded. "But who will watch Jack?"

"He's coming back to the penthouse with me," Cristiano said gravely, "for a little father-son time."

He'd looked at her steadily, as if daring her to object. Hallie had felt it was some kind of test. "But," she said helplessly, "how will you know what to do?"

"I'll keep your diaper bag. Bottles, diapers. Everything I could need, right?"

"Right," she said doubtfully.

He lifted an eyebrow. "I run a billion-dollar company, Hallie. I think I can handle watching my own son while he sleeps for a few hours."

Put like that, she'd been forced, reluctantly, to agree. Giving Jack one last kiss on his plump cheek, she'd slowly gotten out of the SUV. Then she'd turned back anxiously. "I'll be back in two hours."

"Take all afternoon. Take as long as you want. Enjoy yourself. We'll be fine." Leaning forward, Cristiano had given her a goodbye kiss that had left her knees weak, and then he'd smiled. "Have fun."

And, somewhat to her surprise, Hallie had. For the last hour, she and her friends been pampered like royalty at the designer bridal store. Cristiano had already won the loyalty of both her friends.

Tess admired him for demanding marriage immediately. "It's so romantic, practically an elopement! And next he's whisking you off to Italy!" She'd sighed. "So romantic!"

Lola had liked that Cristiano had left them an open credit line and told her and Tess, as bridesmaids, to get new outfits, as well. "Even shoes!"

The bridesmaid dresses were already chosen. Looking at herself now in the mirror, Hallie knew that this wedding dress was the one. It fit her perfectly, no alterations required, and made her look, as Tess had said, like a princess.

Nervously she charged it to Cristiano's account, half expecting the manager to laugh in her face. Instead, the manager rang it up, then talked her into also buying demure white high heels, an elegant veil and bridal lingerie that made her blush. Once all her purchases had been packed and sent off to the penthouse, the three girls headed next door to spend a precious hour at the day spa.

"This is the life," sighed Tess, stretching out her legs as a pedicurist massaged her feet.

"Who's watching Esme, Tess?"

The redhead gave a guilty smile. "My cousin. Don't get me wrong, I love being with my baby. But a few hours to myself feels like a vacation."

"Yeah," Lola said, selecting a chocolate-covered strawberry from a nearby silver tray. "This fiancé of yours is not so bad."

Hallie snorted. "You're just saying that because he told you to spare no expense on the bridesmaid outfits."

"I want your wedding day to be perfect," Lola said demurely, rubbing her heavily pregnant belly as she smiled at the shopping bag that held her new thousand-dollar shoes.

"I just wish Lacey could be here," Tess sighed. "We tried to invite her."

"Lacey!" Hallie smiled at the memory of the energetic young woman who'd invited each of them to the single-moms group, then introduced them to one another. "I owe her a lot."

"Me, too. Because of her, I got to meet you losers." Lola's smile was fond. She held up her champagne glass for another refill of sparkling water from the hovering spa attendant. "Lacey's traveling the world happily with her husband and baby. She sends her love. And promised to send a wedding gift."

"I don't need a gift."

"Of course you don't," Lola said. "You're marrying one of the richest men in the world."

"She doesn't care about his money," Tess protested. She turned to Hallie, her eyes shining. "It's love that brought you together. Pure, perfect love. That's the only reason anyone would marry."

"Um," said Hallie, feeling awkward. Love had nothing to do with it. They were just getting married to give their baby a good home. But she didn't want to disillusion Tess, who was looking at her with dreamy, happy eyes. It made Hallie feel uneasy. She'd told herself that there was nothing wrong with a loveless marriage. Their arrangement would be both practical and sensible.

So why did her throat close at the thought of explaining that to her friends?

"Your baby's father reacted just like I said he would. As soon as he knew about Jack, he realized he loved you and begged you to marry him," Tess said joyfully. "So who knows? Maybe my baby's father will do the same."

"Give it up," Lola said, rolling her eyes. "He's never coming back, Tess."

The redhead sucked in her breath, looking like she was going to cry.

"We don't know that," Hallie said loyally, though she understood Lola's irritation. For as long as they'd known her, Tess had spoken constantly of the man who'd seduced her and disappeared. She'd spun out endless reasons why he might not have returned—ridiculous reasons, like his plane crashing on a desert island, or being kidnapped in Antarctica, or that he'd developed amnesia.

Privately, Hallie agreed with Lola. The guy was obviously a jerk and gone for good. But telling Tess that seemed like kicking a puppy.

Hallie gave the redhead a sympathetic smile. "It could happen, Tess. He could come back."

Her friend gave her a grateful smile. "You think so?"

"Stop encouraging her," Lola snapped. Unlike

the other two, she'd never once spoken of the man who'd gotten her pregnant, no matter how many times they'd asked. "It'll just hurt her more in the end."

"Shush," Hallie told her, and turned to Tess. "He— What's his name again?"

"Stefano," Tess murmured. She blushed. "I never learned his last name."

"Stefano." Where had she heard that name recently? She tried to remember, then gave up. Hallie leaned back in her spa chair, closing her eyes. "He could be on his way to you already."

But as the facialist covered her eyelids with cool cucumber slices, a faint hint of memory teased her. Where had she heard that name?

"This is nice," Lola said, and sighed from the next chair. "You should put something about spa days in your prenup, Hallie."

"My what?" Hallie yawned.

"Your prenuptial agreement."

"Cristiano hasn't asked for one."

"He will. Trust me. Rich men always look out for themselves. He'll want a legal contract. Read your prenup carefully."

"A contract for marriage? That's silly," Hallie said, already half-asleep as the pedicurist massaged her feet. "Marriage is forever. We're going to take care of each other."

Two hours later, as Hallie walked back through the soaring lobby of the Campania Hotel, she felt so relaxed she glowed. For the first time since Cristiano had taken her virginity and kicked her out of the hotel, she felt…happy.

Cristiano had done that, she realized. He'd arranged everything.

He was so different from the selfish, arrogant bastard she'd once thought him to be. He'd gotten her the simple gold ring she wanted, instead of the enormous diamond. He'd invited her friends to join her for a spa afternoon. He hadn't once said the word *prenup*. And, even now, he was taking care of their baby.

"Hallie!"

She turned around, and all the relaxed, good feelings in her body fled.

Cristiano was sauntering through the lobby with a briefcase, Luther behind him. Coming up to her, he kissed her cheek softly. "Did you have an enjoyable afternoon?"

"Yes." *But where—where was—* Hallie looked all around with rising panic, her eyes wide. Her heart lifted to her throat. "Where's Jack?"

Cristiano gave a low laugh. "Upstairs in the penthouse. Safe. In the best of hands."

"Whose?" she choked out. "Why isn't he with you?"

Cristiano started walking toward the elevator, in no particular hurry. "I had to go to my lawyer's office, to collect the prenuptial agreement."

"The *what*?"

His handsome face looked down at her quizzically. "The prenuptial agreement, *cara*. Of course we must have one."

Hallie's jaw tightened. Turning away, she pushed the elevator button multiple times. When the elevator finally opened, she rushed inside. He followed her, frowning.

"Are you in a rush?"

"How can you ask me that?" She frantically tried to push the button for the penthouse floor, but it didn't work until he placed his finger against the keypad, after which the elevator door slid closed.

"Are you upset at the idea of a prenup? You surely cannot think I would marry you without one, exposing me to the risk of New York's divorce laws and the possibility of losing half my fortune."

She whirled on him. "You think I care about money?"

He looked at her evenly. "Everyone cares about money."

"You left our son with a stranger!"

Cristiano's shoulders relaxed. "He could hardly come with me to the lawyer's office. But you don't need to worry. I left him in the care of the best nanny in the city."

He didn't get it, Hallie realized. She'd been a fool to let herself be lulled into trusting him with her baby, even for an afternoon!

Her fears proved right. Even before the elevator opened on the top floor, she could hear her baby crying.

Wailing.

With no one apparently trying to comfort him.

Hallie rushed to the penthouse door. She was ready to kick it open, to scratch it with her hands. "What kind of home is this if I can't even open my own door?" she said furiously.

Wordlessly Cristiano opened the door with his fingerprint, and she rushed through it. Her baby's crying came from the guest room, but as Hallie rushed forward, a stern older woman in a uniform blocked her path.

"Get out of my way," Hallie thundered, pushing past her into the bedroom.

Picking up her tiny sobbing infant from the crib, she held him close to her heart, whispering and singing softly. The baby's wails subsided. Once she'd sat down in the glider and loosened her top, the baby was able to suckle, and his crying stopped abruptly and completely.

"You're making a mistake," the uniformed nanny said, watching dispassionately from the doorway. "It is a mistake I see with many of my ladies. If you give in to your baby's demands now, you'll be his slave. The only way to have a calm household is to get the child on a feeding schedule. You must let him cry it out, madam."

"Cry it out? Cry it out!" Hallie had never been much for swearing, but she suddenly let loose every curse she'd ever heard from her father, who'd been a coal miner and a serious overachiever in the field of swearing. "I'll cry *you* out!"

The woman blanched. "I was hired by Mr. Moretti himself," she said unfeelingly. "I have worked for princes and kings, and I am not going to be insulted by the likes of you."

"Get out," Hallie said, cuddling her baby.

"I'm not going to take orders—"

Her voice became shrill. "Get! Out!"

"Do as she says," Cristiano said in a low voice from behind the nanny, who whirled to face him. His dark eyes glittered in the shadows.

"Fine," she said stiffly. "But I expect to be fully paid for—"

"You'll be paid," Cristiano said. "But if you ask for a reference, don't expect any more princes or kings to hire you."

The woman left with a sniff. Cristiano went to Hallie, who was still sitting in the glider, trembling as she cuddled their baby. He put his hand on her shoulder.

"I'm sorry," he said quietly. "She came highly recommended."

Hallie took a deep breath. She had to force her voice to remain calm. "You have no experience with children."

His eyes flashed to hers, and his expression changed.

"No," he said finally.

She lifted her chin. "You have to learn."

His grip on her shoulder tightened infinitesimally.

"I was told she was the best in New York."

"The best? He was hungry and she was deliberately choosing not to give him a bottle!" She glared up at him. "How can I trust you after this? You convinced me to leave the baby in your care. *Yours*, Cristiano. Not some stranger's!"

For the first time, he looked uncertain. His arms fell to his sides as he muttered, "I told you. I had something to do."

"Yes—watching our son! The son you supposedly care about so much that sharing custody wasn't enough for you—you had to demand marriage! You insisted you wanted to be a father. Was that all just a lie?"

"No," he ground out.

"So why would you immediately desert him?"

"I did not desert him!"

"If you don't want to actually raise him, then what are we even doing?"

Folding his arms, he paced three steps. "You are being unreasonable."

Hallie took a deep breath. "No," she said steadily. "I'm not. If you want us to live with you...if you want me to be crazy enough to marry you tomorrow, then—" she lifted her chin "—I'm setting some rules."

He looked at her in disbelief. "*You're* setting rules?"

"Yes." She added coolly, "We'll even put them into that prenup of yours if you like. Just to make it all official."

He stared at her, clawing his hand through his dark hair. "Fine," he said, his eyes glittering. "Tell me these ridiculous rules."

"First. You will stop being so afraid of the baby."

"Afraid?" he said incredulously. "I'm not afraid!"

"You will learn to be a father to Jack," she continued, ignoring him. "You will learn how to hold him, change him, give him a bottle and bath and rock him to sleep."

His expression darkened. For a second she thought he would refuse. Then he said tightly, "Continue."

"Second. We will spend time as a family. You will join us for at least one meal every day—no matter how busy you are with your company."

"I don't intend to neglect you and Jack," he ground out. "Why would you want that in the prenup?"

Hallie looked at him evenly. "I don't intend to divorce you and steal half your fortune. But, strangely, you still want that written up in a contract."

His jaw looked so tight she wondered if he was hurting his teeth. "Fine."

"I prefer dinner, but if you have to work late, breakfast or lunch is all right, too."

"Anything else?"

Hallie glanced down at her tiny baby son, who had already fallen asleep in her arms. She thought of all her hopes, all her dreams. Only one really mattered.

"Third," she whispered. "You will love him and protect him with your life. As I do."

He stared down at her in the shadowy quiet of the guest bedroom.

"I accept your terms," he bit out. Going to his briefcase, he removed a legal document ten pages long. After turning to the last page, he scribbled something. He handed her the papers.

"Read," he said. "Then sign."

Hallie skimmed the document swiftly, elated to see he'd written all three of her rules exactly as she'd wanted, squeezing them in above the signature lines. As she read through the rest of the pages, the tiny font and legal jargon started to swim before her eyes.

Read your prenup carefully.

The memory of Lola's voice floated back to her,

and Hallie wondered if she should get a lawyer to explain the details to her. But she didn't know any lawyers, and it all seemed like too much trouble when she just wanted to snuggle her sleeping baby and maybe take a nap herself, right here in the chair.

Besides, what was the point of getting married if she couldn't even trust Cristiano? He'd admitted his mistake. He intended to rectify it. She could forgive him. She wanted them to be a family. She wanted security for her son, and a home. Why else would she agree to a loveless marriage?

He'd agreed to her own rules. If he followed them, why would they ever divorce?

But, as she started to sign her name, she heard the echo of Tess's voice.

It's love that brought you together. Pure, perfect love. That's the only reason anyone would marry.

She hesitated, then gripped the pen. Her hand shook a little as she signed her name. She gave him back the document.

"Here," she said a little hoarsely.

"Thank you." His voice was clipped. Setting the papers down on the end table, he signed them without another word.

Hallie wondered what he was thinking. His handsome face seemed closed off, remote.

A rush of insecurity went through her. Were they making a mistake? In settling for a loveless marriage, were they just being practical—or were they selling their souls?

She swallowed and looked up at him. "Cristiano, are we doing the right thing?"

Straightening, he stood over the glider, looking down at her and the sleeping baby in her arms. His voice was cold. "What do you mean?"

"Settling for a loveless marriage…"

"Don't second-guess it," he said harshly. "The decision is made."

He turned away.

"Where are you going?" she said, astonished.

Cristiano stopped at the doorway, his handsome face in shadow. "I have work to do."

"Tonight?" Hallie yearned for him to give her reassurance—a kind word, a smile. "Can't you take the evening off? Tomorrow's our wedding."

"I have taken too much time off already. There are details to finalize before I leave New York."

"But—"

"Get some rest. After the wedding reception, we'll leave for Rome." His voice was brusque, as if she were one of his employees and he was giving her instructions. "You know how to order room service. I'll see you in the morning."

With that, he left, closing the door behind him.

Hallie shivered, looking out the window into the early-evening light, cradling her sleeping baby in her arms.

She should have been proud of herself for standing up to him over the prenuptial agreement and setting her own terms. Instead, she felt as if she'd just agreed to the terms of her employment.

Stop it, she told herself angrily. Once they were married, they'd be a family. Jack would have a secure home. His childhood would be happy, as Hallie's had been.

But something didn't feel right.

With a deep breath, Hallie pushed the feeling away. Tomorrow, she would leave the only country she'd ever known and set off into the unknown.

Tomorrow, she would be Cristiano Moretti's bride.

"Do you, Hallie Jane Hatfield," the judge intoned, "take this man to be your lawfully wedded husband?"

Cristiano looked down at Hallie as they stood

in a quiet, elegant salon on the third floor of his hotel, with chandeliers, a frescoed ceiling and high windows that overlooked the wide avenue below.

"I do," she said, her face pale.

Cristiano's eyes traced over her voluptuous figure in the deceptively simple ivory satin wedding gown. Her dark hair was pulled back beneath a long, elegant veil. She held a bouquet of pink roses. Her beautiful brown eyes were emotionless.

"Do you, Cristiano Moretti, take this woman to be your lawfully wedded wife?"

"I do," he said, and marveled that he didn't have trouble speaking the words. He'd always thought making a lifetime commitment would feel like facing a firing squad. But he felt nothing.

Everything about this wedding had been easy. His executive assistant, Marcia, with the help of the Campania's stellar wedding planner, had pulled the ceremony together in twenty-four hours, so quickly and quietly that the paparazzi had no idea.

Just a few guests were there to mark the occasion. Hallie's two best friends were bridesmaids, each dressed simply in blue and holding a single rose, as requested by the bride. Two babies were also in attendance—tiny newborn Esme, the daughter of the redheaded bridesmaid, and Jack, who was dressed in a miniature tuxedo and held by the other bridesmaid, the pregnant blonde.

His own friend, Ares Kourakis, was there as best man. The Greek owed him that much, as Cristiano had once blindly supported him through a similar endeavor. His bodyguard, Luther, was there with his girlfriend, and Marcia was with her husband. Even Clarence Loggia, the manager of the hotel, had brought a date.

But looking down at his bride, Cristiano had eyes only for her. His gaze traced to her full breasts, pushed up against the bodice of the bias-cut satin, and his body stirred. Angry as he was, he still wanted her.

Last night, when she'd demanded he agree to her rules, he'd been astonished. His original pre-nuptial agreement had been entirely appropriate, standard among the wealthy. He'd assumed Hallie would sign it without demur. Instead, she'd demanded that he add clauses legally forcing him to learn to take care of their child and always come home for dinner. Seriously?

He didn't necessarily have a problem with either of those things. But he wanted them to be requested, not required. No man wanted to be blackmailed by his own wife the night before the wedding.

And then, as if that weren't enough, once he'd signed, she'd wanted emotional reassurance that their marriage was a good idea. With the wedding arrangements made and the gold rings bought, she'd wanted him to waste another night rehashing the reasons for their marriage!

Cristiano had seen many last-minute hardball negotiating tactics in the business world. He'd just never expected them from the mother of his child.

Hallie had gotten what she wanted. What more had she hoped to accomplish last night, asking for reassurance? Had she wanted to hear him beg?

Not in this lifetime. Cristiano glowered down at her.

"Then, by the power vested in me by the state of New York, you are now husband and wife. You may kiss the bride," the retired judge finished happily.

Hallie's emotionless gaze flashed up to his, the sweep of her dark eyelashes fluttering against her pale cheeks. She was breathing rapidly, and he noted the quick rise and fall of her breasts.

Cristiano was already hard for her. His hands

tightened. There would be no more pleading, no more reasoning.

Hallie was his now. Forever.

After a year, his restraint could end. At last, he could claim his prize.

He pulled her into his arms. Lowering his head, he crushed his mouth to hers.

Their lips joined in a flash of heat that ripped through him like a fire. She gasped, then her resistance melted and she kissed him back, matching his desire with her own. As her hands reached up around his shoulders, he heard her bouquet fall to the floor.

The guests applauded and whistled. He took his time, relishing his possession.

When he finally let her go, Hallie's deep brown eyes were shocked and wide. She looked dizzy as they turned to face the cheers of their friends. Stepping forward, she stumbled and he grabbed her arm to steady her. The truth was, though he was better at hiding it, he felt exactly the same way. He wished they were alone so he could take her straight to bed. As it was, he had to adjust the coat of his morning suit to hide the blatant evidence of his desire.

While they accepted the congratulations of their

well-meaning friends, Cristiano hummed with impatience. As they enjoyed lunch in a private room of his hotel's elegant restaurant, it was all he could do not to tell his friends to get the hell out.

Midway through their friends' champagne toasts, Cristiano could take it no longer. He cut them off, rising to his feet.

"You'll have to excuse us," he said perfunctorily. "My bride is tired, and needs time for a nap before our flight to Rome."

Everyone looked at Hallie, who appeared astonished.

"Thank you for coming," Cristiano said firmly. Rising to his feet, he reached his hand out to Hallie. "Please feel free to stay as long as you want and order whatever you like." He turned to the pregnant bridesmaid, who was holding Jack. The baby was happily smiling and clapping his hands. "Would you mind watching the baby for an hour?"

"Sure," she said, a glint of wicked amusement in her eyes.

As he pulled his new bride out of the private dining room, he saw the bridesmaids look at each other with a knowing grin, and even Ares Kourakis gave him a smug smile, as if to say, *See? It happened to you, too.*

Cristiano didn't give a damn. After all this time, Hallie was his wife. She was his by right.

He intended to make her so—in every way.

"You were rude," Hallie snapped once they were alone in the elevator. He pushed the button, then turned to her.

"Do you want to go back and make my excuses?" he said in a low voice, running his hand softly over her ivory satin wedding gown, up her arm, to her neck, to her sensitive earlobe and her cheek. He felt her shiver.

"You're a brute," she whispered.

"Yes," he growled. "And now you're mine."

"I'm not—"

Lowering his head, he cut her off with a rough kiss. Pressing her against the wall, he cupped her breasts, kissing down her throat. With a soft gasp, she surrendered, closing her eyes as her head fell back. With her in his arms, he was lost in a sensual haze. He'd almost forgotten they were in an elevator when he heard the bell ding and the door slide open on the top floor.

Lifting her in his arms, he carried her into the penthouse, kicking the door wide over the threshold. Once inside the bedroom, he set her down on her feet, letting her body slide slowly over his so she could feel how hard he was for her.

"Mrs. Moretti," he whispered, and felt her shiver at hearing her new name. In front of the windows revealing the shining New York skyline, with deliberate slowness Cristiano pulled out the pins holding her veil. Her lustrous dark hair fell tumbling down her shoulders.

"You're so beautiful," he said hoarsely.

Reaching up, she loosened his tie. Her brown eyes were soft and inviting. Tossing his black morning coat on the white sofa, he pulled her in his arms.

"You're mine now, Hallie," he said, fiercely searching her gaze. "You know that, don't you?"

"Only if you admit you're mine."

"Yes," he whispered. "Forever."

He lowered his mouth to hers, crushing her body against his own. Sensation and yearning and desire ripped through him, and in that moment he simply let go.

Let go of his anger. His self-control. His reason. He let go of his need to guard himself from everyone and everything.

All that mattered was her.

All that mattered was this.

He slowly unzipped her wedding dress, letting it drop to the floor. He took a ragged breath when he saw her in her wedding lingerie—a white lace bra and tiny panties that clung to her deliciously full hips.

Lifting her up with a growl, he lowered her reverently onto the bed.

Never taking his eyes off her, he loosened his platinum cuff links and unbuttoned his white shirt, then dropped it onto the floor. Pulling off his black trousers, he climbed beside her on the enormous bed, pulling her against his body.

"I've wanted you so long," he whispered.

Her eyes were luminous, and, like a miracle, she lifted her lips to his.

A rush of overwhelming need poured through him, and he crushed her violently against his hard body, plundering her mouth with his own. He yanked off his silk boxers, intending to roll her onto her back and push himself inside her, to impale with a single thrust.

Then he remembered that he had to be gentle. Even though his body was raging with the need to take her, she'd just had his baby three months before. A low curse escaped his lips. He might be a brute, but he wasn't a…a *brute*.

Gentling his embrace, he lingered, naked against her lingerie-clad body, kissing her slowly and thoroughly. Their tongues touched and intertwined in their kiss until he heard her soft sigh, until he felt her body rise. He stroked her face, lightly kissing her forehead, then caressing slowly down her cheek to suckle her ear. He gloried as he felt her shiver beneath him.

Moving down her body as she lay stretched on the bed, he cupped her breasts over the white lace, then with agonizing slowness, removed her bra. He nearly groaned at the sight of her magnificent breasts. He felt their naked weight, before he kissed down the sharp crevice between them, down to the sweet slope of her belly.

For a moment, he teased her with the warmth of his breath. Then he moved lower, and lower still. Finally, gripping her hips, he lowered his head between her legs, teasing her thighs with his breath.

Her hands gripped his shoulders, as if she were afraid of what he might do next, or afraid he might stop.

He ran his tongue along the edge of her white lace panties, letting the tension build in her. Then he ripped the lace off her body entirely.

Lowering his head, he tasted her, caressing her

with the hot, slick pressure of his tongue. As she gasped beneath him, he spread her thighs wide with his hands. Ruthlessly, he pressed his mouth against her hot wet core, working the taut nub of her pleasure with his tongue. She gasped, then held her breath.

Then…she exploded.

Fierce joy filled him at seeing her ecstasy.

Moving quickly, he covered her naked body with his own. Lowering his head, he pressed his lips to hers, swaying his hips sensuously against hers. Still lost in pleasure, she accompanied him, her body rising anew. With deliberate slowness, he positioned himself between her legs. He watched her face, keeping himself under control as he finally pushed inside her, filling her inch by delicious inch. He heard her shocked gasp of pleasure. She wrapped her hands around his shoulders, pulling him down harder against her. And, with a groan, he obliged her, thrusting deeper until he was all the way inside her, all the way to her heart.

He was deep, so deep inside her.

Still dazzled by the pleasure he'd given her with his mouth, Hallie moaned softly as he entranced her anew, filling her so completely. She tried to remember when she'd ever felt such intense pleasure. Even their first night together, as incredible as it had been, hadn't been like this. What was the difference? Was it that they were wed, bonded together forever as man and wife?

Or was it something more, something she felt in the deepest corner of her soul—that he belonged to her, and she to him?

But, as he filled her so slowly and deeply, it wasn't just her body that ached desperately for release.

She wanted to love him.

That was the one thing she couldn't do. The one thing that could only lead to ruin: loving her husband.

For a moment, she looked up at his handsome face looming over hers, at his heartbreaking dark eyes. She closed her eyes, turning away as he kissed slowly down her throat.

Slowly, deliberately, he began to ride her. And all she wanted was more. She gasped, clutching at the white comforter beneath her, wrapping her legs around his hips. His thrusts seared her, hard and deep.

Gripping her shoulders, he pushed into her with increasing roughness until their bodies were sweaty, their limbs tangled. Her fingernails tightened into his shoulders, her back rising off the bed, until she exploded, flying even higher than before, higher than she'd ever imagined. Pleasure overwhelmed her in waves so intense she almost blacked out.

With a low growl, he thrust one last time, then roared as he exploded with her.

Gasping, they clutched each other, eyes closed. She struggled to catch her breath. He collapsed beside her, holding her as if she were the only thing that existed. They held each other, tangled in the shadowy bed, for what could have been minutes or hours.

When Hallie finally opened her eyes, she saw Cristiano was pulling away from her, sitting up.

"Don't leave," she pleaded, reaching for him. "We still have a few hours."

He smiled down at her, taking her hand and kissing it tenderly. "It would be good to arrive in Rome early. My jet is already waiting. We should go."

"But our friends…"

"Our friends will understand." Leaning down, he kissed her naked shoulder with a sudden wicked grin. "And there's a bedroom on my jet."

Shivering with need, exhausted with desire, Hallie grinned at him. She blushed, shocked at her own wantonness.

Lowering his head to kiss her one last time, he whispered, "You are magnificent, Mrs. Moretti." Getting up from the bed, he headed for the en suite shower.

Once he left her, she felt suddenly cold, bereft. She wanted him back in bed. Beside her. For always. And not just that.

With an intake of breath, Hallie realized how easy it would be to give her husband—the man who'd told her outright that he could never love her—not just her body, but her soul.

CHAPTER SIX

As the Rolls-Royce drove from the private airport into the crowded and winding streets of Rome, Hallie's head was twisting right and left. She knew she was gaping like a fish, but she didn't care.

After five years in New York, she'd thought no city could easily impress her; yet she'd never seen anything so beautiful, so decadent, so ancient, as the Eternal City.

She looked out the window at a red sports car zipping by, at a young girl in a scarf clinging to a smiling boy on the back of a cherry-colored moped. Down the street, she saw a passionate young couple gesticulating angrily at each other in front of a sidewalk café, before the man swept the woman up into a hungry kiss.

Roma. Hallie felt the city like a thunderbolt. It was like, she thought, a huge, sexy party, with food, wine and dancing—all on top of an ancient tomb. The city itself seemed to cry out: *Take every bit of joy today, for someday you will not be at the party, but below it.*

"What do you think?" Cristiano looked at her over the baby's seat in the back of the limo.

She shivered at the frank sensuality of his gaze. She could hardly believe that she was his wife. Cristiano was her husband. Good thing, too. What he'd done to her last night...

After their passionate interlude at the penthouse, they'd made good use of that bedroom on his private jet. Any time the baby slept, he drew her into his bed, into shockingly sensual delights so new she still shook at the memory.

He smiled, his eyes amused, as if he knew exactly what she was thinking about.

Blushing, she turned back toward her window, marveling as their Rolls-Royce sped down slender, crowded roads, following traffic laws she didn't understand. They'd been met at the airport that morning by their new Italian driver, who was called Marco, and new bodyguard, Salvatore. She gaped as they drove past one incredible ancient monument and cathedral after another. Finally, they arrived at the Campania Hotel Rome, a magnificent Mediterranean-style edifice near the top of the Spanish Steps.

Tilting back her head, she gaped when she got out of the Rolls, staring up at the glamorous hotel. She held her breath as she turned to see the view. All of Rome was at their feet.

"Like it?" Cristiano murmured lazily.

"I've never seen anything like it."

"Of course you have not." He grinned, looking pleased. "Campania is the best luxury hotel brand in the world. And the Campania Roma is the best of them all."

As Marco and Salvatore collected their bags, Hallie and Cristiano strolled hand in hand. Baby Jack, pushed by his father in the stroller, didn't seem nearly as impressed by their surroundings. He chewed on the stuffed giraffe clipped to his shirt.

Hallie looked down at the letters imprinted on a manhole cover near the sidewalk. "What is SPQR?"

"It's Latin. *Senatus populusque Romanus*—the Senate and People of Rome. You'll see the emblem everywhere in the city."

"Wow. This city is really old," she said in awe, and flashed him a grin. "Almost as old as you."

He lifted an eyebrow. "Am I old?"

She liked teasing him about the eleven-year difference between them. She countered, "You're teaching me Latin now?"

His dark eyes simmered. "Let me take you to our room, *cara*. And I'll teach you other things. All night long."

Her cheeks burned as a smiling, dark-eyed doorman held open the hotel door. Pushing the stroller ahead of them, they walked into the soaring lobby.

Hallie sucked in her breath. The opulence was unbelievable. Gilded Corinthian columns stretched up toward the Murano glass chandeliers high above.

"I didn't think it possible," she breathed. "This place is even more amazing than your hotel in New York."

He smiled at her. *"Grazie."*

She turned to stare as a chic fortysomething woman passed by, dressed to the nines in six-inch heels and a velvet skirt suit so well crafted the jacket was like a corset, and perfect scarlet lips. At the woman's side was a man in a well-cut suit who paused to let his eyes caress Hallie before he continued past. Hallie blinked in amazement, staring after them. "And the people..."

"What about them?"

"All the women look like movie stars. And the

men like James Bond. Everyone dresses as if they're about to meet the love of their lives. What is this place?"

Cristiano gave her a sudden wicked grin. "Roma."

She shook her head in awe at a city where everyone, from teenagers to octogenarians, seemed to claim eternal sensuality as both a privilege and a duty. "You grew up here?"

"I lived here briefly."

She knew so little about his past. "You were born in Rome?"

His gaze shuttered, as if he could sense her probing.

"Naples," he said flatly. Clearly he wasn't interested in saying anything more.

Mr. Moretti was a brawler, back when he was young. He fought his way out of the streets of Naples.

His driver's words came back to her. Not for the first time, she wondered how a fatherless, penniless boy, neglected then orphaned by his mother, had made his fortune, turning himself into an international hotel tycoon.

"Look." Cristiano pointed at the lobby ceiling. She gasped, tilting back her head to look up.

On the ceiling, gold-painted stars decorated

a midnight sky. Across the lobby, she saw huge vases filled with red flowers beside marble fireplaces carved with cherubs. The enormous sweeping staircase had an actual red carpet.

She'd never seen anything so incredible, not even in a movie. She stopped, feeling she was in a dream. "It's—it's—"

"I know," Cristiano replied. "The building was once a *palazzo* gone to ruin. I was only twenty-two when I convinced the *contessa* to sell it. It took two years to rebuild and restore it. I gambled everything I had—my reputation, my future. This place," he said softly, looking around them, "was the making of me."

His voice was deep with emotion. Hallie looked at him, her heart in her throat.

Coming back to himself, he smiled at her. "Come."

As they walked through the hotel lobby, everyone beamed at Cristiano, and not only him.

Somehow, weirdly, everyone in the hotel seemed to already know Hallie. As if, simply by marrying Cristiano Moretti, she'd suddenly become a celebrity in her own right—famous, beautiful and adored. They all beamed at her.

"Buongiorno."

"Buongiorno, signor e signora."

"Benvenuto, Signora Moretti."

After three different people of different ages greeted them, Hallie turned to Cristiano in bewilderment. "They know who I am?"

He gave her a crooked grin. "Of course they do. We were married yesterday. By now everyone in Rome knows you are my wife. You're a celebrity here, *cara*."

"Why would I be a celebrity?" Then, looking at his face, she gave him a sheepish grin. "You're teasing me."

"I don't tease," Cristiano said. Taking her hand, he brought it to his lips for a brief, hot kiss, then whispered, "At least not that way."

She shivered until he released her hand.

"Be serious," she pleaded. She saw several people in the lobby covertly lifting cameras to take her picture. Why? Was something wrong with her? She looked down at the simple outfit that Cristiano's concierge had packed for her in New York. It was sleek and severe, less comfortable than her beloved sundresses: a black dress with a sweetheart neckline and black high heels.

Cristiano had assured her that the outfit would be appropriate in Rome. Now, her heart pounded at all the curious eyes staring at her. "Why is everyone looking at me?"

"Because many Italian women want to know your secret."

"What secret?"

His dark eyes flickered. "Of how you hooked me into marriage."

"Um, by letting you accidentally knock me up?"

With a snort, he said mildly, "In New York, I am not that unusual. There's a Sicilian tycoon in my hotel who is a well-known playboy, in addition to being a cold bastard. Even Ares Kourakis, my best man at the wedding, was called uncatchable before he fell for some little waitress from the West last year. But here, in Rome and Naples, everywhere in southern Italy, I am famous." He looked down at her, caressing her with his eyes. "And now, so are you."

Butterflies skimmed through Hallie. As he led her to the extravagantly gilded elevator, and they rode it to the top floor, the butterflies only increased. Marco and Salvatore went ahead of them, carrying their luggage.

Cristiano stopped at the penthouse door with the stroller. "Welcome to our home."

"Our home?"

He smiled. "For now."

Following him inside, Hallie saw a large suite of rooms, all decorated as lavishly as the lobby. The baby's blue-walled room was furnished with every luxury and comfort, with books and lavish toys. Next to that, she saw the enormous master bedroom, with a huge bed and walk-in closet.

Through sliding doors, she walked out onto a terrace. Purple flowers laced the edge of the railing and she felt the hot Italian sun beating down from the blue summer sky. Looking out, she gasped at the panoramic view, gaping in wonder at the old buildings, domed churches and Roman temples spread out across the seven hills.

Coming from behind, Cristiano wrapped his arms around her, pulling her back against his chest, nuzzling her neck.

"It's so beautiful," she whispered, and turned around in his arms, feeling she was in a dream.

He smiled. "You're beautiful, *cara mia,*" he said huskily, lowering his head to hers. "And now that you're my wife, I intend to give you the world..."

For the next two weeks, whenever Cristiano wasn't working, checking every detail of this hotel—which had prepared strenuously for his inspection—he took Hallie and the baby to explore the city.

First, he insisted on taking Hallie shopping. With the new burly bodyguard at their side, they visited all the grand shopping streets of Rome, starting with the expensive boutiques near the Spanish Steps.

"More shopping?" she'd protested in dismay. "Is that really necessary?"

"One must be conscious of *la bella figura* in Rome. Even more than in New York. And it will help you relax, knowing you fit in."

"How would you know?" she grumbled. "You fit in everywhere."

Looking at her, he said quietly, "I came to Rome as a young Napolitano. I changed my clothes and changed my fate."

Hallie waited breathlessly for him to continue, to tell her more of his hard childhood and how he'd made his fortune. But he did not.

Sighing, she gave in, rolling her eyes. "Fine. Take me shopping."

She was relieved when the clothes were purchased and they could do what she really wanted—explore the city. They bought Jack a wooden sword and shield at the Colosseum and laughingly tossed coins in the Trevi Fountain. They drove past an enormous white-columned building that looked like a wedding cake, and the endless Roman ruins scattered around the city as casually as food carts in New York.

In the evenings, they had room service sent up to their penthouse for dinner, but once Cristiano took them out, to a simple outdoor trattoria with a private courtyard near the Piazza Navona. As the sun set, with flowers everywhere and foundations burbling, Hallie wistfully watched musicians sing and play guitar, remembering her old dream of a singing career. Cristiano had observed her, then had a quiet word with the trattoria's owner.

A moment later, the musicians spoke into the microphone and invited Hallie to come up on stage and sing. Embarrassed, she'd tried to refuse until Cristiano had said, "Please, do it for me."

Staring at his handsome face, she couldn't deny anything he asked of her. She'd gone up on stage and sung an old Appalachian folk song a capella.

Applause rang in her ears as she returned to their table. As she passed by, an American man claiming to be a record executive even gave her his card. Laughing, she showed it to Cristiano when she sat back down at the table.

"I told him thanks, but no thanks. My days of trying to get singing gigs are over."

"Are you sure?"

Remembering all the painful years of rejection, she nodded fervently.

"Good," he said huskily. "You'll sing only for me."

For the rest of the evening, Hallie ate pasta and drank wine and watched her new husband learn to be comfortable holding their baby. Seeing Jack tucked gently and tenderly in Cristiano's arms, she felt a rush of happiness, like everything was right with the world.

But once they left the trattoria's private court-yard, Salvatore had to hold back the rush of on-lookers and paparazzi eager to take pictures of their family. It made her scared to go out on the street with the baby.

Each night, she sang lullabies to Jack, the same lullabies her mother had once sung to her, passed down from her grandmother and great-grandmother before. That night, when her baby finally slept, with his plump arms over his head, she turned and saw Cristiano silhouetted in the doorway, his face in shadow.

"Those songs you sing," he said in a low voice. "They break my heart."

Drawing her out of the nursery, he kissed her and pulled her to their bed. Then he made her heart break, too, with the purest happiness she'd ever known.

However, after living in a hotel for two weeks, she'd started to feel trapped, unable to leave the penthouse without Cristiano and the bodyguard.

One afternoon while he was working, Hallie took her baby out onto the penthouse terrace to enjoy the warm summer sun. Watering the purple flowers that decorated the terrace railing, she tried to pretend she was back in West Virginia, in their old garden. Her mother had loved to spend hours taking care of their plants. As she watered the flowers, she would sing.

"Why did you never leave, Mama?" Hallie had asked her once in the garden, the year before she'd died. Hallie had just graduated from high school, and what the world was telling her she should want and what she actually wanted seemed to be two different things. "Why did you never go to New York and become a famous singer?"

"Oh, my dear." Turning to Hallie, her mother had caressed her cheek tenderly. "I did think of it once. Then I met your father and traded that dream for a better one."

"What?"

"Our family." Her mother's eyes had glowed with love. "Your whole life is ahead of you, Hallie. I know whatever you decide to do, you'll make us proud."

And so, after she'd lost everything—her mother and father and brother and home—Hallie had taken her father's meager life insurance and gone to New York. To try to make her family proud.

"Hallie?"

Lost in thought, standing on the terrace watering the flowers, Hallie jumped when she heard Cristiano's voice behind her.

Turning, she saw him, devastatingly handsome as always in a sleek suit. He wasn't alone. Behind Cristiano was an older woman, plump, white-haired and simply but perfectly dressed.

"*Cara*, I have someone I'd like you to meet." He looked over Hallie's tank top and capri pants as she stood holding a glass pitcher from the kitchen. "Are you watering the flowers?"

She could hardly deny it, since he'd caught her red-handed. "Um, yes?"

"You must not. We have hotel staff who are paid

very well to do it and who are supporting families. You would not wish them to be out of a job?"

"I suppose not," she said, crestfallen. With a sigh, she set down the glass pitcher on a nearby table. "I can't wait until we have a house of our own."

He frowned. "A house?"

"When we go back to New York."

"I thought you liked Rome."

"I do, but..." She thought of her friends with a pang. "Tess sent me a text that Lola had her baby yesterday. I miss my friends. I'm looking forward to when we can settle down and have a proper home."

A strange expression crossed Cristiano's face. "Well, we'll talk about that later." Clearing his throat, he motioned to the white-haired woman behind him. "I'd like you to meet Agata Manganiello. She lives in Rome and used to work for me. She was my first secretary, long ago."

"Hello...um...*buongiorno*," Hallie said.

Smiling shyly, the woman said in careful English, "Hello, Mrs. Moretti. I am pleased to meet you."

"I'm pleased to meet you, too," Hallie said, then turned inquisitively to Cristiano.

"I have known Agata for almost fifteen years," he said. "She is careful, responsible. She's very good with children."

"I raised six of my own," Agata said proudly, "while working for Cristiano." She tilted her head thoughtfully. "I think caring for you was harder than the other six put together."

Cristiano gave a good-natured laugh. "You were a miracle worker," he said affectionately.

Hallie looked at him in amazement. He sounded so relaxed. And the Italian woman had called Cristiano by his first name. She'd never heard any of his other employees do that, not even Mr. Loggia, the manager.

Cristiano was treating this woman like…family.

"You're thinking of hiring her to watch Jack," Hallie said slowly. "Aren't you?"

His gaze met hers. "I'd like you to consider it."

"But I don't want a nanny."

"Not a nanny. A babysitter. Occasionally, I'd like to take you to dinner, just the two of us. And once my new hotel opens on the Amalfi Coast, there will be a grand ball to celebrate. We will sometimes need help. And I'd trust Agata with my life."

He waited, watching her. Biting her lip, Hallie

considered. It felt very different from when he'd tried to force that last awful nanny on her by surprise.

Reluctantly she turned to the older woman. "You raised six children?"

Agata nodded. "And now I have five grandchildren."

She has kind eyes, Hallie thought. Cristiano said he trusted her with his life.

Slowly she asked, "Would you like to hold Jack?"

The woman smiled. *"Sì, naturalmente."*

Picking up the baby from the thick quilt on the terrace, Hallie placed him in the woman's capable arms and waited for him to fuss. He simply gurgled happily, reaching a flailing arm toward Agata's nose.

"I was thinking Agata and the baby could get to know each other this afternoon," Cristiano said. "If it goes well, I'll take you out to dinner tonight. Just the two of us."

Hallie opened her mouth to argue. Then she heard Agata crooning some Italian song as she snuggled Jack in her plump arms, to the baby's delight. She looked at them. Jack seemed happy and content.

"I'll think about it," she said grudgingly.

"Va bene." Cristiano kissed her lightly on the forehead. "I will be back in a few hours to spend time with Jack, then you and I will have dinner. As per your rules. Speaking of which—" he angled his head "—I've been thinking about making some new rules of my own."

She frowned. "What rules?"

His smile transformed into a grin. "Wait and see."

Hallie watched the Italian grandmother carefully that afternoon, telling herself she'd send Agata away the instant Jack seemed unhappy. But the baby seemed to love her, and Agata was easy to have in the penthouse, kindly and unobtrusive. It was almost, Hallie realized, like having…no, not her mother, but some kindly great-aunt come to watch the baby. Maybe it was the fact that Cristiano—who didn't trust anyone—seemed to trust her, for it made Hallie trust her, too.

Later that evening, with the baby safely fed and sleeping in his crib, she left capable Agata in charge and went out on a dinner date with her husband for the first time.

Hallie dressed carefully in a new, sexy black dress with a bare back that he'd bought her. Trying to match the drama of the dress, she pulled her long, dark hair into a high ponytail that hung down over her naked back. Going to the internet for makeup tips, she lined her eyes with black kohl and mascara to make them smoky and dramatic, then put on scarlet lipstick.

As she came out of the bedroom, she was nervous that Cristiano wouldn't like her new look.

But, when he saw her, his jaw dropped.

"You make me want to stay home," he growled, coming closer. In his own well-cut black buttondown shirt and trousers, his dark hair rumpled and sexy, he looked amazing to her, as always.

"Please, take me out," she whispered.

"As you wish." Catching her hand in his own, he lifted it to his lips. His breath against her skin made her shiver all over. "I'll take you out." He gave her a sensual smile. "Then I'll take you in."

He never let go of her hand as they descended the elevator into the lobby. Past the crowds, she saw a bright red Ferrari waiting for them in front of the hotel.

"What about Salvatore?" she asked, looking at the two-seater car.

"I want to be alone with you tonight," he said, opening her door.

As Cristiano drove her through the streets in the fast sports car, she looked out her window at the sensuality of Rome at night. So mysterious and dangerous, the city seemed to whisper two words: *sex* and *death*. She felt his hot gaze on her. Then he punched down hard on the gas, racing over the hills of the city.

Eventually he parked in front of a nineteenth-century brick building tucked back on a quiet street. There was no sign it was a restaurant except for two valets standing mysteriously in front.

"What's this?" she asked as he helped her out of the car.

Cristiano smiled. "It's by invitation only."

Once inside, a maître d' escorted them through the building and out into a lush garden courtyard. Scattered at ten small tables, she saw people she recognized—famous performers, politicians and athletes. Her eyes widened as they walked past someone that Hallie knew had millions of social-media followers.

"What is this place?" Hallie whispered to Cristiano. His hand tightened on her arm as other patrons turned to look at them with similar interest.

"A Michelin-starred chef runs the restaurant

as a hobby. He invites only friends, or friends of friends."

She looked at the ruined walls on the other side of the courtyard. They looked ancient. "How old are those?"

Cristiano glanced casually at the ruins. "Fifth century, I'd imagine."

They were escorted to the best table, beside an old stone fountain. She looked up. The only ceiling was the dark velvet of the Italian sky, twinkling with stars. Fairy lights were strewn against the rough, ruined walls, illuminating red flowers and greenery proliferating amid the cracks.

"Incredible," she breathed.

Cristiano reached for her hand over the table. His gaze was hungry. "You're incredible."

After fully enjoying each other every night over the last two weeks, she felt deliciously sore all over. And aware. So aware. Just his hand on hers made her body tighten and shiver. When the tattooed waiter spoke to Cristiano in Italian, she thought again how easy it would be to love her husband.

But she couldn't. It would be a horrible mistake. Because he would never love her back, and, eventually, that would make her love turn to hate.

Their meal started with a cocktail, the ubiquitous Aperol spritz, a light bubbly drink blending Prosecco, soda water and orange liqueur over ice and orange slices, but with an added twist of rosemary. Sipping the drink, Hallie felt the other celebrities staring at them. She glanced down at herself self-consciously. She whispered, "What's wrong with me?"

"Why do you think something's wrong?"

"Why would they—" she waved her arm toward the powerful, fascinating people at the other tables "—stare at me?" She bit her lip. "It's my makeup, isn't it? The bare back of my dress? I look weird, don't I?"

He leaned forward. "You are," he said huskily, "the sexiest woman in Rome."

She felt the weight of that compliment and saw, from the expression in his eyes, that he meant every word.

As their eyes locked, a pulse of heat rushed through her. Turning away, she took a sip of the light, bubbly cocktail to try to cool down. She cleared her throat. "But there are so many beautiful people here. Famous people. Why would they bother looking at me?"

"You're famous now, too. And unlike all of

them—" he dismissed his fellow patrons with a glance "—no one knows anything about you."

Hallie gave an incredulous snort. "I'm just a regular girl from rural West Virginia."

Wordlessly Cristiano drew his phone from his pocket. Pressing a few buttons, he handed it to her.

Hallie stared down at the screen in amazement.

"See? You're a star," he said softly.

Looking at his phone, she realized it was true. Pictures and stories about her had exploded all over the internet. She was on news websites. Celebrity gossip pages. Someone had started a fashion blog in Italian, with a photo of her every time she'd come out of the hotel over the past two weeks, with a listing of each day's clothes, who'd designed them and where to buy them. There was even a page devoted to Jack's clothes. Her baby had somehow become a fashion icon.

It was jarring to see pictures of herself, taken without her knowledge, and pictures of her baby, too, all now online for the world to see.

She sucked in her breath when she saw a video of herself singing at the trattoria, posted on YouTube a few days before. It had already gotten over a hundred thousand hits. *A hundred thousand.*

Her mind boggled.

But not all the attention was positive. Some of the posts were downright mean. Strangers were calling her a gold-digger. And, apparently, Hallie's family tragedy made excellent news fodder. Many news stories breathlessly reported that Hallie was a failed folk singer from a poor Appalachian family who'd all died tragically in a flash flood, but then she'd gotten pregnant and was now married to an Italian billionaire, so wasn't she the luckiest girl in the world?

The words and pictures swam before Hallie's eyes. Her stomach clenched. Abruptly she gave him back his phone.

"You see why," he said quietly, "I want you always to take Salvatore with you when you're out on the street."

Hallie shivered. As a girl, she'd wistfully dreamed of growing up to be somehow special. Hadn't she even gone to New York hoping to become a star?

Now she found that being the center of attention just made her uncomfortable. Feeling the warm night breeze against the bare skin of her back, she tried to smile. "You didn't bring Salvatore with us tonight."

"This restaurant is exclusive. The patrons are

mostly famous themselves." His eyebrow lifted. "Besides, I can protect you."

Remembering the night he'd forced her landlord to return her precious possessions, Hallie could well believe it. Biting her lip, she ventured, "Matthews said that you were a street fighter in Naples when you were young."

His expression closed up. "That is one way of saying it. I had no money. So I fought."

"And now you are a billionaire, with the most luxurious hotel chain in the world."

"So?"

"How did it happen? How did you build your fortune?"

Cristiano stared at her, his handsome face shadowed against the soft lighting of the garden.

"I was lucky," he said flatly. "I met a man who owned a small hotel chain in southern Italy. I convinced him to hire me and teach me everything he knew. Then I betrayed him."

Shocked, Hallie stared at him. With a cold smile, he took a sip of his drink, then looked up as the waiter arrived and, in both Italian and English, listed the five choices on the evening's menu.

Cristiano ordered the veal, Hallie the *spaghetti alla vongole*—pasta with clams in a light wine sauce. She added, "And could I get that with lots of Parmesan cheese, please?"

Both Cristiano and the waiter stared at her with identical horrified expressions.

"Clams…seafood…these you should not eat with cheese," the waiter said patiently, as if explaining to a toddler she shouldn't run into traffic.

Hallie smiled, but held her ground. "I still like them."

"But it is not done!" The waiter looked at Cristiano for support, but he just shrugged, as if to say, *Americans, what can you do?*

When the pasta arrived, Hallie covered it with Parmesan and thought it was delicious. She washed it all down with a glass of red wine, causing another shocked gasp from the waiter, at the thought that she'd drink red wine with seafood, not white. Hallie decided that maybe she enjoyed shocking people, because she didn't care.

As the evening lengthened, a pleasurable sensation seeped into her bones. Maybe it was the delicious dinner or the sensual wind against her bare skin. Maybe it was the fragrance of the flowers or sitting with Cristiano amid a fifth-century ruin beneath the starry sky. But she felt strangely like she was in a dream.

"When are we going back to New York?" she asked.

"I'm not sure." Cristiano watched her. "After I'm done in Rome, I'll need to go to the Amalfi Coast for a few weeks to oversee the finishing touches on the new hotel opening in Cavello. The grand opening gala is next month."

She brightened. "I've always wanted to see the Amalfi Coast."

"You and the baby will remain in Rome. I'll commute via helicopter."

"What? Why?" she said, dismayed. More weeks spent cooped up in the penthouse, afraid to go out alone on the streets of Rome didn't sound appealing. A prison was a prison, no matter how luxurious. "That's not what the rules say. What about our family time?"

"Rules are made to be broken."

"Not my rules. You gave your word."

He ground his teeth. "I cannot bring you with me. The Campania Cavello isn't yet ready for guests, and I can hardly let it be known that Cristiano Moretti's bride is staying in a rival's hotel."

"That would be bad," she agreed. She looked down at her empty plate. "Still, you must find a way," she said in a small voice. "I don't want to be separated from you."

"You won't be." His leg brushed hers beneath the table, and she looked up. The air between them changed.

Sitting across from Cristiano in the sexy black dress, defying the tattooed Italian waiter and even her own husband to enjoy her meal exactly as she pleased, Hallie realized she wasn't the same shy girl she'd once been. She felt stronger. Braver.

Becoming Cristiano's wife, living in Rome, wearing this sexy dress, with dark eyeliner and bright red lips, she felt bolder somehow. She didn't know why, but she suddenly felt powerful. Like his equal.

Maybe that was what gave her the courage.

"I need to know when we can go back to New York and buy our own house."

Taking a bite of veal, he frowned at her. "We have twenty-two houses."

She blinked, taken aback. "You mean your hotels?"

"Yes." He swirled his wineglass. "The hotels. All of them fully staffed in the most beautiful locations. The perfect way to live. We never need to settle. We'll never get bored. And I can run my company and build my empire."

"Your hotels are amazing, but…" How could she say it? "They're not home."

"A home, a home," he repeated irritably. "I'm tired of hearing you ask about it."

She looked at him in surprise. "I've barely mentioned it."

"For days now, all the lullabies you sing to Jack have been about finding home and losing home and longing for home."

She drew back, genuinely surprised. "Really?"

He scowled. "Plaintive, heartbreaking folk songs. Are you trying to wear me down?"

"I didn't realize…"

"From now on, sing happy songs to our baby," he ordered.

"Okay," she said, biting her lip. The songs she knew were mostly old Scottish-Irish ballads, a repertoire that didn't exactly specialize in "happy" songs. "Um… I'll try to think of some."

"And we don't need to buy a house. You should be happy living all over the world in penthouse suites with spectacular views, waited on hand and foot by staff. That should be enough."

She paused.

"It's…nice," she said carefully. "For a honeymoon. But we need a permanent place of our own. Maybe with a garden."

"A garden? In Manhattan?"

"They exist," she said defensively. "I worked once at this amazing house on Bank Street. There was a garden tucked in back."

"By *garden*, do you mean a few pots on a stoop?"

"A real garden," she said indignantly. "My employers let me go because the owners lived overseas and were never there. They were going to put it up for sale."

"We would never be there, either," he said. "My work requires constant travel, and I want you with me."

"But soon Jack will go to school…"

"Truly you think our son is a prodigy if he needs to go to school when he has not yet learned to roll over."

Defiantly Hallie lifted her chin. "You talk about building an empire. I want to build a family." She hesitated. "I'd prefer New York, but I can compromise. If you want to live in Italy, I can make it work. I'll learn Italian and try to make friends—"

"We're not staying. After the new hotel is

launched in Cavello, we'll spend a few weeks in Tokyo, then Seoul, Sydney and Mumbai."

"All those places," she said faintly. Beautiful places she'd only imagined. Normally she would have been thrilled at the thought of seeing them with her own eyes. But tonight, she thought longingly of her friends. Lola's baby, now one day old. "After that, we'll go back to New York?"

"Briefly. Then Paris, London and Berlin." He paused. "I have twenty-two hotels, and they all need my attention."

Her heart sank. Circling the world, she would barely see her friends. And forget about a garden. Her eyes fell forlornly to her plate. "Oh."

Cristiano scowled at her. "Surely you're not complaining about traveling around the world in a private jet, staying in luxury hotels."

But a life of luxury had never been Hallie's dream. Licking her lips, she said, "I'm sure all those places are amazing, but…"

"But?"

"How can we ever have a home if we never stay in one place for long?" Her voice was small. "How will I make friends? How will Jack?"

"Learn all the languages, as I have. Be a citizen of the world."

"A citizen of nowhere."

"Everywhere," he corrected coldly.

Angry tears lifted to Hallie's eyes, though she didn't want to fight, not on their first baby-free date. She tried to keep her voice calm.

"Traveling is fine, but eventually we need to stop and have a home!"

"What you call home I would describe as a prison. I'm not buying you a house, Hallie. It would be a waste of money."

The warm summer night suddenly felt cold.

"So you'll waste money on everything but the one thing I actually care about?" Folding her arms, she turned away stonily. By now, as the night grew late, many of the tables had emptied.

"Hallie." His voice changed, turned gentle. "Look at me."

Grudgingly she did and saw his dark eyes were tender.

"Tell me why a house means so much to you," he said. "Because I truly do not understand."

Hallie took a deep breath.

"The house I grew up in was built by my great-grandfather. By his own two hands." She tried to smile. "The songs I sing to Jack, the songs you love so much, they were the ones my mother once sang to me. My family lived for generations on the same mountain. I had close friends. A place in the world."

"If you loved it so much," he said quietly, "why did you leave?"

With an intake of breath, she looked away as a rush of pain filled her heart. Even after five years, grief often still caught her like this when she wasn't looking. "Everything was suddenly gone. My family. My home. I couldn't stay. I felt lost." Her hands twisted together in her lap. "My parents always said I should be a singer. Even my brother said it. So I tried. For five years."

"That's a long time."

She gave a choked laugh. "So many people try to break in as singers in New York. All so talented, better than I'll ever be."

"I doubt that very much."

"The harder I tried to succeed, the worse I felt." Looking down, she said softly, "And it didn't bring them back."

Silence fell across their table. She heard the clank of silver against china from a few remaining patrons and the distant sound of traffic and birds crying in the night.

"So why," Cristiano said slowly, "would you

ever choose to leave yourself vulnerable to such pain? After losing so much, I'd think you'd never want a home again."

Hallie looked at him. "Is that why you live in hotels?" she said softly. "Never stopping. Never staying."

Cristiano's eyes widened slightly. Then he drew back, his jaw tightening. Rising to his feet, he held out his hand. "Come. The night is growing cold."

It was quiet in the sports car as he drove them back through the city after midnight.

How did you build your fortune?

I was lucky. I met a man who owned a small hotel chain in southern Italy. I convinced him to hire me and teach me everything he knew. Then I betrayed him.

Hallie looked at him sideways, wishing she had the courage to ask him who the man was and why Cristiano had betrayed him. She stayed silent.

Before their wedding, she'd convinced herself he was a good man, deep down. But now that they were married she was starting to see a darkness inside Cristiano she'd never glimpsed before.

She was suddenly afraid of learning things about him she didn't want to know.

When they arrived back at the hotel, they found Jack sleeping in his crib and Agata snoozing nearby on the sofa, her knitting folded neatly in her lap. After they'd thanked her and she'd left for the night, Hallie and Cristiano tiptoed into the darkened nursery. For a moment, they just stood together looking at their slumbering child.

Then Cristiano took her hand. Wordlessly he led her to their bedroom, and even though a corner of her heart was still angry, she could no more resist him than stop breathing.

Once in their bedroom, he pulled her against him. In the slanted moonlight coming through the blinds, his eyes burned through her. So did his fingertips, lightly stroking down the top of her sexy black dress, the bare skin of her back.

"I have followed all your rules, have I not?" he said in a low voice.

Confused, Hallie nodded.

"I've shared a meal with you both every day? Learned how to care for our son? Loved him?"

"You know you have."

"Now it is time for you to learn some lessons, also." Pulling her close, Cristiano nuzzled her throat, kissing the sensitive hollow at her shoulder before suckling the tender flesh of her earlobe. She shivered beneath his touch. Her heart was pounding.

"L-lessons?"

He stroked his hand along her cheek, rubbing his thumb against her lower lip. "How to truly please me."

Hallie's eyes went wide. "Have I not pleased you?"

He placed a single finger against her lips.

"You have, *cara*," he said huskily. "But I want more. Not for me. For you."

"There's more?" she whispered.

He smiled. "Even after two weeks of marriage, you are still so innocent." His hungry eyes met hers. "I will teach you how to know what you want and how to get it. I will teach you," he whispered, cupping her cheek, "how to experience a different level of pleasure entirely."

He kissed her, leaving her breathless and clinging to him. Reaching back, he pulled out the elastic of her ponytail, and her dark hair tumbled down her bare back. Roughly he yanked down her black sleeveless cocktail dress, dropping it to the floor. She stood shyly before him in only her tiny black lace panties, her naked breasts heavy and full.

With a low growl, he pushed her back against the window. Behind them was a vision of Rome, the sweep of cathedrals and Roman ruins spread across the hills, illuminating the darkness at their feet.

"The first rule is," he said in a low voice, "don't hold back."

He pushed his knee between her bare legs, gripping her wrists against the window as he kissed down her throat. She gasped with pleasure.

This is wrong, she thought, *so wrong*. Anyone could look up and see them through the window. She should put a stop to this. Be modest. Be…

Sensual kisses caused swirls of pleasure to cascade down her body. She wanted more. She wanted to wrap her arms around him, to feel him.

The first rule is don't hold back.

Yanking her wrists from his grasp, she folded her arms around his shoulders, drawing him against her. She kissed him back hungrily, matching his fire. But unlike her, Cristiano was still fully clothed. It didn't seem fair.

Grabbing the top of his shirt, she ripped it down the front, scattering buttons against the floor. She sighed in pleasure as her hands roamed the warm satin of his skin over the hard muscle of his chest, laced with dark hair. She squeezed his nipples and luxuriated in the sound of his gasp, followed by a low masculine growl.

He wrapped his hands over the back of her black lace panties, which had cost three hundred euros at a very nice lingerie shop on the Via Condotti. As she felt his hand move forward between her legs, she was wet and aching. Pulling him closer, she kissed him hard.

With a growl, he ripped off the black panties, leaving them a pile of crumpled lace on the floor.

"Please," she whispered. Amazed at her own boldness, she reached down to unzip his black trousers.

He gave a jagged intake of breath. With a single motion, he pushed down his silk boxer briefs. Using both hands, he lifted her backside, pushing her up against the window, as her legs wrapped around his hips.

Then he pushed inside her with a single, deep thrust.

Feeling him so thick and hard inside her, she moaned, closing her eyes and letting her head fall back against the glass. Her hair tumbled around them as she gripped his shoulders. As he moved, she didn't care anymore who might be watching.

She didn't even pause to wonder if the window could break. She knew only she couldn't let him stop.

Her arms wrapped around his shoulders as he pumped inside her, hard and fast. Her full breasts pushed against his hard muscles, the hair of his chest rubbing against her sensitive nipples. She gasped with pleasure as, with each thrust, he filled her more deeply. Her legs tightened around his hips as she built higher and higher until, with a gasp, he exploded into her the moment she screamed his name.

Screamed quietly, of course, so as not to wake the baby. Even lost and frantic with abandon, though she might have been willing to risk shattering the window to fall to her death on the streets of Rome, she wasn't going to risk waking their sleeping infant. She was wanton, she was bold. But she wasn't insane.

For long moments afterward, sweaty and panting for breath, they held each other, collapsing against the enormous bed, their naked bodies intertwined.

"All right," Cristiano said in a low voice.

"What?" she said sleepily, lifting her head from his shoulder.

His expression was blank, his handsome features half-hidden in shadow. "I'll buy you a house."

Joy filled her heart. "You will?"

"But you must let me choose where."

"I don't even care where," she lied, pushing away her longing for her friends in New York. What difference did the location make? As long as their family had their own place with a garden, and they could live in one place long enough to make friends and really settle in, what did she care?

"You won't be sorry," she said tearfully. "We'll be so happy. You'll see. You won't regret it."

Cristiano looked at her, his eyes glittering in the shadows. "I regret it already."

CHAPTER SEVEN

CRISTIANO RARELY DID things for others, and he never did anything he did not want to do.

But perhaps there was something in do-gooding after all. Because the moment he decided to buy a house to please his wife, he'd discovered one for sale on the Amalfi Coast that was spectacularly satisfying for him to acquire. Especially at a cut-rate price.

Just weeks after he'd made his promise to her, their Rolls-Royce approached the magnificent estate on the rugged cliffs of the Amalfi Coast a short distance from the village of Cavello. A wave of euphoria went through Cristiano.

It was his.

He remembered the first time he'd passed through this same tall wrought-iron gate, surrounded by old stone walls. He'd been young then, newly orphaned, utterly penniless. And obsessed with revenge.

Luigi Bennato had been kind from the beginning. Strange for a man who'd ruthlessly rejected his infant son, in order to focus on building his small luxury hotel chain. But Cristiano had been coldly determined to impress him. And he had. Bennato had seen something in eighteen-year-old Cristiano, something no one else had.

But he didn't detect everything. He didn't see that Cristiano was his long-abandoned son.

Why would he? Even if he'd remembered Cristiano's mother, her name then had been Violetta Rossi. *Moretti* was the name of the man who'd been her husband when Cristiano was born. Her first husband. Her second husband had been an Englishman, her third an American. Both horrible stepfathers, whose only gift to Cristiano had been teaching him English. After a third screaming divorce, his mother had given up on marriage and focused on love affairs that were increasingly short, violent and toxic.

But Luigi Bennato was the man who'd destroyed her first. According to Violetta, before she'd met him, she'd been an innocent virgin who'd never tasted wine. Bennato had seduced her, then tossed her out of his life when she'd fallen pregnant and refused to have the abortion he demanded.

His mother had told Cristiano the story repeatedly when he was growing up. She'd always ended it the same way. "And Luigi was right," she'd say with a swill of bourbon and a raspy cough. "I should have done what he wanted. Then I'd be happy!"

After his mother's death, eighteen-year-old Cristiano had stood at her grave and felt nothing. What kind of man would feel nothing at the death of his own mother?

It was then that he knew himself for a monster.

But, standing in the rain, he'd had a new thought, one that lit a fire deep inside him. One that made him feel warm for the first time in his life.

Revenge. He had let the word settle against his lips, caressing it like a lover.

Vendetta. He'd loved the rhythm in his mouth.

Rivincita. He'd felt his tongue brush softly against his teeth.

He would have his revenge on the man who'd first made his mother a monster, so she in turn could make one of Cristiano.

And he'd had his revenge. In just three years, Cristiano got his vengeance. He'd claimed the ruined *palazzo* in Rome for himself, with Luigi's rival as his investor. He'd left Luigi's company in tatters.

Cristiano marked his adulthood from that moment. His revenge had been the act that had defined his life. The first step on a path that had made him richer than his wildest dreams.

The truth was it had been almost too easy. He still couldn't believe how quickly and completely Bennato had trusted him. It was almost, he thought sardonically, as if the man had *wanted* to be destroyed.

Now Cristiano was more powerful than Luigi Bennato had ever been. He was famous. Better in every way.

It still wasn't enough. Some part of him craved more, wanted to crush the ashes of the man's life smaller still. Which was why he'd chosen Cavello as the site of his newest Campania Hotel.

The old man's business had long since gone bankrupt, without enough capital to refurbish the hotels to satisfy the constant demands of perfection that a wealthy clientele required. Bennato's three small luxury hotels, once the jewels of Capri, Sardinia and Sorrento, had all long been demolished and replaced.

Several times over the years, Luigi had tried to contact him. Cristiano had never responded. He had no interest in listening to the man's angry recriminations. Let the man figure out for himself why Cristiano had destroyed him.

It was now seventeen years after he'd first entered the stately villa once owned by Bennato, and Cristiano had bought it for himself. The bankrupt, lonely old man was living in the former housekeeper's tiny house outside Cavello.

Life could be full of unexpected joys, Cristiano thought with satisfaction. As the Rolls-Royce pulled up in front of the grand courtyard of the elegant nineteenth-century villa, he smiled to himself, glancing at Hallie, waiting for her reaction.

Her eyes were huge as she looked from the villa to the terraced, manicured gardens overlooking the sea. *She's in shock*, he thought smugly. He was already keenly anticipating the sensual expressions of her gratitude later.

Their driver, Marco, opened the door and helped Hallie out of the car with the baby. Behind them parked an SUV carrying Agata, Salvatore and all the luggage.

Hallie's mouth was open as she looked out over the vastness of the estate, which had once been owned by the King of Naples.

"Welcome to your new home," Cristiano said. He waited for her cries of joy, for her to fling her arms around him and kiss him with the intensity of her delight.

She simply held their baby, looking up blankly at the palatial villa.

"Our home," he said encouragingly. "Just like you wanted."

Looking at him, Hallie shook her head. "This wasn't what I had in mind at all."

"It's the grandest house on the Amalfi Coast. What can you possibly dislike?"

"It's too big."

"Too big?" he said incredulously. How could anything be too big?

Hallie looked at him. "It's like a hotel."

"We'll be the only ones living here."

"We'll need a megaphone to find each other."

He frowned. "And the gardens—what do you find wrong with those?"

Slowly she looked around the manicured gardens, from the formal hedge maze to the perfectly arranged flowers and palm trees overlooking the blue Tyrrhenian Sea.

"It's…like a park," she said. Turning back to face him, she shook her head. "How can I possibly take care of it all?"

"We'll have staff, of course."

"Oh." She looked oddly dejected. Not exactly the reaction he'd been hoping for.

"Would you prefer a sad, broken-down apartment?" he said shortly. "Where you can hear neighbors screaming and your windows get smashed by thieves? Where the electricity is often out and even your few, most precious possessions can disappear at any moment to pay for—"

For your mother's whiskey, he'd almost said. He caught himself just in time.

"No. Of course not." Putting her hand on his arm, Hallie gave him an apologetic smile. "You're right. I'm being a jerk."

He didn't respond. He was suddenly picturing his mother the last time he'd seen her. Violetta's face had been bruised and bleeding from her lover's fists, and she'd been screaming at Cristiano for trying to defend her. That was his last memory of her face. He'd returned hours later to find her house ablaze.

He could still feel the searing pain of the flames when he'd nearly died trying to get inside to save her. He could hear the crackle of the fire and the furious howl of grief that rose to the dark sky when they brought her body out of the embers and ash.

"I'm so sorry." Feeling Hallie's hand against his cheek, he focused on her again. "I've made you upset, haven't I?"

"No," he bit out.

"I can see I have. I'm sorry for sounding so ungrateful. The house is beautiful. Thank you."

Reaching up on her tiptoes, she kissed him. Taking her roughly in his arms, he kissed her back hungrily until their baby, still held on Hallie's hip, complained about the close quarters, and they both pulled away with rueful laughs.

Tilting her head back to look at the palatial villa, she said, "I'll try to get used to it."

Cristiano took her hand. "Come see inside."

As they walked through the long hallways, over the tiled floors and past the antique furniture and tapestries, Hallie obligingly oohed and aahed over every detail he pointed out. Having gotten over the initial shock, she seemed determined to be pleased.

He'd arranged for new furniture to be put in the master bedroom and the baby's nursery next door. Finally they walked out onto the villa's wide terrace and Hallie approached the railing. Beneath the hot August sun, hungrily she drank in the incredible view as soft sea breezes lazily blew ten-drils of her hair.

"Wow. Maybe this place isn't so bad." With a laugh, she glanced back at him with sparkling eyes.

But Cristiano didn't return her smile. As he looked out at the magnificent view of the sea and the village clinging precipitously to the rug-ged cliffs on the other side of the bay, he was overwhelmed by the memory of the last time he'd stood on this terrace. He could still see Luigi's bright eyes, the man's chubby cheeks smiling as he'd said, "My boy, this *palazzo* in Rome, this is going to be the thing for us! It will take our com-pany global!"

Our company, Luigi had said. *Our.* The memory was like a rough piece of cut glass on Cristiano's soul because, after three years of working for the man, Cristiano had started to like him, even re-spect him. Bennato had been generous, kind. He'd treated Cristiano almost like a son.

He shook the memory away angrily. If Ben-nato had wanted a son, he shouldn't have thrown Violetta and Cristiano away like trash. The old man deserved what he'd gotten. Bennato was the one who'd taught Cristiano the lesson: Life meant every man for himself.

And yet, suddenly, Cristiano didn't enjoy owning the villa as much as he'd thought he would. Thinking of the times he'd ignored Luigi's calls over the years, he wondered what the old man would have said.

"The view is incredible," Hallie whispered. She wiped her eyes surreptitiously. "Thank you. You don't know what this means to me. You don't know how I've longed to have a real home where we can stay forever and ever."

He opened his mouth to inform her that after the Cavello hotel opened in two weeks, they would still be traveling to Asia on schedule. He'd bought this house as a temporary amusement, perhaps a long-term investment. But he doubted they'd return to Italy for another six months, or perhaps even a year.

As he looked down at her, though, the happiness in Hallie's face made him change his mind. Her caramel-brown eyes glowed at him.

He didn't want her to stop looking at him that way.

"You're welcome," he said softly, taking her

hand. Together they looked out at the picturesque rocky coastline plummeting into the blue sea.

Later that night, as they slept together in the palatial master bedroom, with the windows open to salty sea breezes scented with tropical flowers, Hallie made him very, very glad that he'd made her so happy.

But he could make her happy anywhere, Cristiano told himself afterward, as she slept so contentedly in his arms. He had nothing to feel guilty about. Yes, he'd bought her a house. He'd never promised they would stay.

Cristiano looked toward the terrace, toward the moonlit sea. His arms tightened around his wife. He had promised himself long ago never to sacrifice his own needs for another's. And he never would.

Life meant every man for himself, he thought. Even in marriage.

After just two weeks of living in her new home on the Amalfi Coast, Hallie felt she had fallen into sunshine and joy.

She sang all the time. Songs about dreaming of love and falling in love and being in love.

For no particular reason, of course.

Hallie was thrilled to have a home at last. A place, as she'd told her husband, where they could stay forever and ever. Even as formal as the villa was, with its endless gardens, the view was breathtaking from every window, looking out with a sharp drop to the sea. And when she went outside the villa's gate, no one bothered her here. No paparazzi. No fashion bloggers sneaking pictures of Jack. Here, Hallie could just be herself.

It was true that Cristiano hadn't been around much. He often worked eighteen-hour days, personally overseeing the final touches of the lavish new hotel in Cavello, on the opposite cliff, while still running his worldwide empire.

And if he'd broken her dinner rules a few times, disappearing from the house before dawn and not returning until well after midnight when she and Jack were asleep, well, she'd decided to bend the rules. He was busy. Hallie could understand. He'd given her what she wanted most—a home, and she'd tried to be flexible. She hadn't even complained.

But she was relieved it was almost over. Tonight, the Campania Hotel Cavello would have its grand opening gala, and then Cristiano would be able to spend more time in their new home. They could finally be together as a family.

His constant absence had to be why, in spite of the beauty and comfort, this villa still didn't feel quite like home to her. Maybe it would just take time. But she still didn't have the feeling of home she'd had as a child, living with her family in the rickety wooden house in the mountains.

True, there was a staff of four to oversee the house and gardens. It sometimes made her uncomfortable having servants cook and clean and pull weeds for her, but she'd told herself she'd get used to it. She should be grateful. All she had to do was care for her baby, decorate her home as she pleased, bake cookies if she felt like it, and water any flowers she wished.

Still, in spite of being surrounded by servants and having Jack with her, sometimes her days felt lonely.

Since they'd arrived on the Amalfi Coast, she'd seen Cristiano only at night, in the dark, when he woke her up to set her body on fire with bliss. Then, in the morning, when she woke, he was always gone. Like some tantalizingly sweet dream.

Strange she should feel lonely when she was never alone. Even when she walked to the village with the baby, Cristiano insisted she take Salvatore with them. It bewildered her because there were no paparazzi here, and it was hard enough trying to make new friends, given her lack of Italian, without also having a hulking bodyguard standing behind her, scowling behind his sunglasses.

But the villagers were friendly and interested in meeting the wife of the man who'd brought so much new employment to the area. And baby Jack, with his bright smile and chubby cheeks, charmed everyone he met, even on the rare occasions when he cried.

Hallie was slowly learning Italian from Agata, who was very patient with her. Living in a brand-new country where she didn't speak the language, she was trying her best to settle in, make friends, to find a dentist and doctor and grocery store, and do everything she could to make the Amalfi Coast feel like home.

Except for the wistful memory of her childhood home, Hallie didn't miss West Virginia. She missed New York. But she tried to push that feeling away. Hadn't she told Cristiano that their home could be anywhere? If Italy was the place he loved most, then she would be happy here. She would try to forget New York, especially since every time she tried to text or phone Tess and Lola lately, they seemed distracted. No wonder, with newborns.

But she missed their friendship.

The afternoon before the gala, Hallie played with Jack in the huge formal salon, kissing his fat baby feet as he lay stretched out on a blanket beneath a flood of afternoon sunshine. Soon, Cristiano would come home and they'd get ready to go to the gala together. As she sang yet another song about true love, she knew tonight would be magical. After tonight, their lives could truly begin.

Her voice suddenly choked off as she realized she did know happy songs after all. Love songs.

Wide-eyed, Hallie looked out the wide windows at the palm trees and blue sky. She stared down at her cooing baby, his dark eyes exactly like Cristiano's.

And she gasped aloud, covering her mouth with her hand.

There was a reason she'd been singing only happy love songs lately.

Because she felt them.

She was in love with Cristiano.

Her husband. Her ex-boss. The man she'd once

hated. The man she'd never thought she could trust.

She trusted him now. He'd become a real father, a real husband. He'd brought her home. He'd given her what she'd dreamed of most: *a family.*

She loved him for everything he'd done for her. For the way he'd made her feel. For the person he'd encouraged her to be. Bold. Fearless.

Was she fearless enough to tell him she loved him?

Hallie gulped.

If she did, would his handsome face light up? Would he say, "And I love you, *cara mia,*" then kiss her senseless?

Or would he just look at her coldly, and say nothing?

Love had never been part of the deal. Cristiano had told her outright he didn't think he was capable of it.

Yet, he treated her as if he did love her. Marrying her. Buying her this magnificent home. Giving up his lifestyle of constantly traveling in order to remain here, in one place. Just to make her happy.

She put her hand on her forehead. What should

she do? Should she remain silent and keep things safely as they were?

Or should she take the chance and risk everything in their marriage to tell him she loved him?

"It's just arrived from Rome, *signora*," said Agata, coming into the salon with a designer garment bag in her arms.

"The dress," Hallie said, rising unsteadily to her feet. "Cristiano told me he'd called in a favor with a designer, to send me a special dress to wear tonight."

"Sì." The Italian woman didn't meet her eyes, but Agata had been acting strangely all day. Taking the garment bag from her, Hallie laid it across the elegant sofa. Unzipping the bag, she discovered a breathtaking strapless red ball gown with a sweetheart bodice and full skirts. It was a dream dress. A Cinderella dress.

Hallie touched the fabric in awe.

"Maybe he does love me," she whispered.

Agata made a strange noise.

"What?"

The Italian woman cleared her throat. "Cristiano told me not to say anything. He intends to tell you himself."

"Tell me what?" Hallie said, holding up the

beautiful red gown and looking at herself dreamily in the mirror. Maybe she'd tell him she loved
him tonight, while they were dancing at the gala.
If she could just be brave enough, maybe she'd be
rewarded. Maybe against all odds, he'd pull her
closer in his arms and—

"You are a good woman, *signora*. What he is
doing is not right, keeping it from you."

Hallie turned in bewilderment. "What are you
talking about?"

"Then again, I understand why he hates this
house and wants to be away as soon as he can."

Hallie sucked in her breath. "Cristiano doesn't
hate this house!"

The older woman looked at her sadly. "He does,
signora. Because of the man who used to own it."
She turned away. "And that is why, while you are
at the ball tonight, he has ordered me to pack all
your things. Tomorrow, you leave for Asia. Me,
I have refused to go. I will return to Rome, close
to my grandchildren."

"Leaving?" Hallie drew back. "But we just got
here! It's our home! We're not leaving our home.
And I don't want you to leave us!" Agata had
started to feel like family.

"I'm sorry, *signora*. He said to pack everything," she said quietly. "I doubt you're ever coming back."

Anguish went through Hallie. It couldn't be true.

And, in a flash, she knew it was.

She'd thought Cristiano had changed, that he'd been willing to sacrifice his restless travel for her and actually settle down in one place.

But he hadn't changed at all. This so-called home was temporary, like everything else in his life.

And Cristiano had told Agata first. Before his own wife.

Hallie's hands clenched at her sides. While she'd been trying to compromise, to make this place her home, he'd been lying to her. He'd never intended to settle down at all.

Hallie looked around the villa. This antique furniture wasn't to her taste. It was too big, too fancy, but since they'd arrived, she'd convinced herself to overlook that, so badly had she wanted a home.

Now he wanted to drag her and the baby back to his empty lifestyle of moving from hotel to hotel to hotel?

All she wanted, all she'd ever wanted since her

parents and brother had died, was a home. A family. A place in the world.

Hallie choked out, "If he hates this villa, why did he buy it?"

Agata looked at her sadly, her wrinkled eyes mournful. "He bought it for the same reason he hates it. Because the man who once owned it was his friend, then his enemy. Luigi Bennato was the first to give him a real job. He taught him how to run a hotel. Then Cristiano turned on him. Ruined him."

Hallie shivered as she heard the echo of Cristiano's voice. *I met a man who owned a small hotel chain in southern Italy. I convinced him to hire me and teach me everything he knew. Then I betrayed him.*

She wasn't sure she wanted to know more. In a small voice, she said, "What happened?"

"I worked for Luigi," Agata said. "Before I worked for Cristiano. I still don't understand. For three years, they worked together, as close as father and son. Cristiano used his charm and Luigi's money to convince a widowed countess to sell her *palazzo* in Rome. Then, instead of developing the hotel together as they'd planned, at the last minute Cristiano took the information to one of the international hotel chains. He cut Luigi out of the deal. Left him bankrupt."

Hallie stared at the older woman, cold with shock. "But why?"

"I still do not know. Yet, even after Cristiano betrayed him, Luigi tried to protect him. He even convinced me to accept Cristiano's job offer in Rome. 'The boy's still so young,' Luigi told me. 'He'll need someone he can trust.' So I left Luigi's hotel for Cristiano's. And now he's a broken man. He has no family, no money. He lives in an old shack. I feel badly for him."

"Why are you telling me all this?" Hallie whispered.

Agata looked at her. "He wants to talk to you."

"Who?"

"Luigi Bennato."

Hallie stared at her in shock. "Why would he want to talk to me?"

"I do not know." The white-haired woman looked at her steadily. "All I know is your husband owes him a debt."

Meet the old man Cristiano had betrayed? Hallie felt caught between fear, curiosity and loyalty to Cristiano. "I couldn't. Besides," she said hesitantly, "how do I know he wouldn't attack me or something?"

"Luigi?" Agata gave a low laugh. "He has a good heart. Better than Cristiano's. Luigi is no risk to you. He's waiting in the forest on the other side of the gate."

A trickle of fear went down the back of her neck. "He's here? Now?"

"Tomorrow you leave Cavello, possibly never to return. He might not live until your next visit. I told him I would ask you. If you wish to see him, it is your choice."

Hallie stared at her, a lump in her throat.

"I'll leave you to get ready for the gala. I need to pack for your trip." She sighed. "And my own back to Rome. Tonight will be my last time watching Jack, while you're at the gala." Agata smiled sadly. "I will miss you both."

"Won't you come with us?"

"I'm sorry." The older woman's eyes lifted apologetically. "I do not want to leave Italy. It's my home. My place is here."

Hallie hugged her hard. After Agata left her in the salon, she was still blinking back tears, but she couldn't blame the older woman for not wanting to endlessly circle the globe. Hallie didn't want to do it, either.

She wanted a real home. She wanted to be surrounded by the people she cared about and who cared about her.

She wanted to love her husband, and she wanted him to love her back.

Hallie sucked in her breath. What would she do about Luigi Bennato?

Her eyes fell on her baby, playing happily on his blanket. She couldn't go behind Cristiano's back to talk to the man he'd betrayed. He wouldn't like it. At all.

But then—Hallie's face suddenly hardened—he'd done a few things lately that she didn't like, either.

She picked up her cooing baby. Crossing to the foyer, she grabbed the stroller in quick decision. If Cristiano wouldn't explain anything to her, if he wouldn't tell her about his past or open his heart, she would find out without his help.

If she loved him, she had to try to understand.

"Going somewhere?" Her bodyguard, Salvatore, stood in the doorway, looking at the stroller.

Blushing, she said quickly, "Oh, no, I just wanted to clean the stroller."

"All right. I'm going to lunch."

Hallie waited until the bodyguard had gone into the kitchen to have his usual lunch and flirtation with one of the maids. Quickly she tucked Jack into the stroller, along with a pacifier, a blanket and an extra diaper just in case, and crept quietly out of the villa.

It felt scary and exhilarating to go by herself. She realized that this was the first time she'd gone out alone since the day she'd told Cristiano about the baby, back at his hotel in New York.

Jack cooed happily in the sunshine as she walked swiftly toward the rough stone walls leading to the gate. Around the side, some distance up the hill, she saw an old man peeking through the trees. She stopped, wondering if she was making a mistake.

Gathering her courage, she took a deep breath and pushed the stroller forward.

"Signora Moretti—you are she, yes?" said the old man anxiously as she came forward. He was plump, and his hair was gray, and there was something about him that seemed oddly familiar.

Hallie took a deep breath. "You wanted to talk to me?"

She was startled to see tears in the old man's

rheumy eyes. "Cristiano's wife," he whispered. "I have seen pictures of you." His gaze fell to Jack, who was waving his fat arms, as he whispered, "And his son?"

He'd seen pictures of them? Oh, yes, right—she was famous. "I'm so sorry, Mr. Bennato. I don't know the whole story between you. But I know my husband betrayed you. You must hate him for what he did to you."

"Hate him?" The old man's dark eyes looked strangely familiar. She tried to think who they reminded her of. He shook his head. "I am proud of him for doing so well. I am glad for him to have my villa."

Her lips parted. Surely no one could be *that* kind, no matter what Agata had said. "That is very generous…"

"An old man like me, I don't need a big house." He looked at the baby with longing, then lifted his tearful gaze. "I'm so happy to meet you both."

"But why? After the way Cristiano betrayed you, why would you…?"

Then she looked more closely at the old man's eyes. Black, like obsidian. Like her baby's.

Like her husband's.

"Cristiano's your son," she whispered. "You're the father who abandoned him."

Luigi gave her a tearful smile. "I saw a picture of Violetta in the paper after she died in the fire. Her last name had changed, but I recognized her. When I read she was survived by an eighteen-year-old son, I was desperate to find him. Before I could—" he took a deep breath "—Cristiano himself showed up at my hotel, asking for a job."

"You knew he was your son?"

"I thought…maybe. He looked like I did when I was young. And Violetta had told me she was pregnant with my child. But sometimes she lied to me, especially when she was drinking. One day, I could take it no longer and told her we were through. She said she was pregnant, so I tried to make it work. I made her stop drinking. But she screamed I was making her a prisoner. When she was six months pregnant, she disappeared. I never saw her again."

"Why didn't you tell Cristiano? He thinks his father abandoned him!"

"I did abandon him." The old man's voice trembled. "I tried so hard to find them. But I should have tried harder. I never should have given up. What I read about the life Violetta was living before she died…" He shuddered. "I cannot imagine what that boy went through as a child. When Cristiano showed up at my door asking for a job, he seemed to have no idea I might be his father. He said he just wanted to work at the best boutique hotel in Italy. I thought it was a miraculous coincidence."

"Why didn't you tell him?"

"I decided I couldn't reveal myself as his father, not until I was sure it was true. But I kept putting off the test. I think I was afraid," he said quietly. "By the time I finally stole a hair off his brush and sent it in for the test, it was too late. The day he betrayed me…" His voice trailed off as he looked out at the sea. "That was the same day I got proof he was my son."

"So why didn't you say something?" Hallie cried. He gave her a small smile.

"It was too late. I didn't want to cause him pain. He had no idea I was his father when he betrayed me. And I thought…perhaps I deserved it. So I let him go."

Closing her eyes, Hallie took a deep breath, pain filling her heart. She looked down at her happy baby. She couldn't imagine the pain of losing him. "Why are you telling me all this?"

Luigi gave a wistful smile. "He has done well, my boy. He's built his own hotel empire over the last fifteen years. He's been more successful than I ever was." He blinked fast. "He is my only family. When he refused to answer my phone calls, I tried to accept it. But then I read about him having a wife and child…" More tears filled his rheumy eyes as he gently stroked Jack's head. "He's my grandson. You're my daughter-in-law. But my son…" He lifted his gaze. "Please. You must convince him to speak to me."

Hallie hugged the old man tightly, wiping away her own tears. "I'll make this right," she said softly. "I swear to you."

When she finally returned to the villa, the afternoon was growing late. Hallie was still shivering with emotion and regret. How would she tell her husband that the man he'd betrayed had been his own father?

Her baby had fallen asleep in his stroller so she left him in the foyer when she heard Cristiano calling her from the salon. Nervously she went to see him.

She found Cristiano pacing angrily. When she entered the salon, he turned to her, his expression furious.

"Where have you been?" he said tersely.

She stopped. "On a walk."

"I told you to always take Salvatore!"

"I wanted to be alone." She bit her lip, trying to think of how to break the news to him. She wanted to do it gently and couldn't. Her brain was exploding. "I met your father."

"What?" Eyes wide, Cristiano stumbled back. "What are you talking about?"

"I got a message that a man wanted to meet me. So I went to talk to him." She looked at her husband anxiously. "Perhaps you should sit down…"

He didn't move. "You met my father?"

"I'm afraid this is going to be a big shock." She took a deep breath, then said very gently, "Cristiano, your father is Luigi Bennato."

For a long moment, he stared at her. Then he turned away, his shoulders shaking. At first, she thought he was crying. Then she realized he was laughing. His laugh was harsh and strange.

Hallie stared at him, wondering if the shock of the news had disjointed her husband's mind.

"Don't you understand, Cristiano?" she said in a low voice. Reaching out, she put her hand on his shoulder. "The man you betrayed—he's your father. I'm so sorry. Such a horrible coincidence—"

"Coincidence?" He whirled on her, silhouetted in front of the windows overlooking the sea. His dark eyes glittered. "I knew Bennato was my father. Of course I knew! And from the moment my mother died, I vowed to make him pay!"

Hallie drew back, astonished. She whispered, "You knew?"

"My mother told me how he ruined her life. She was just an innocent girl when he seduced her. He gave her her first drink, and when she got pregnant, he told her to go to hell!"

Hallie thought of Luigi's heartsick face, at the tears in his wrinkled eyes when he said, "I tried so hard to find them. But I should have tried harder. I never should have given up."

"Luigi told me, after Violetta got pregnant," she said slowly, "he tried to make her stop drinking. But she hated that, and she ran away. He said he tried so hard to find you—"

"He was lying," Cristiano said coldly.

She shook her head. "I believed him."

"Of course you did." His lips twisted in a sneer. "A man as devious as Bennato could easily twist your innocent little heart."

His scorn made her shiver. She lifted her chin. "You're wrong. If you'd only speak to him—"

"What else did he say?" He came closer to her, his face like stone. His powerful body left her in shadow.

Hallie saw the cloud of darkness around him, and for the first time she was afraid.

This was the darkness she'd feared. The darkness she hadn't wanted to see.

"You'll never talk to him, will you?" she whispered. "You hate him beyond all reason. You'll never be free."

Cristiano's black eyes narrowed into slits as he repeated dangerously, "What did he say?"

"He regrets not protecting you when you were a child. He's all alone now. He wants to make amends. He wants a family."

"He wants money."

"No." She shook her head eagerly. "If you'd seen his expression when he touched Jack's head—"

"Jack?" His expression changed, then his folded hands dropped to his sides as he roared, "You let him touch our son?"

"Of course I did. He's Jack's grandfather!"

"Don't call him that!" Furious, he turned away. "Where is Jack?"

"Sleeping in his stroller. In the foyer—"

Cristiano strode out of the salon. When she

caught up with him in the foyer, she found him cradling their sleeping baby tenderly against his powerful chest. When he looked up at Hallie, his dark eyes glittered.

"You will never," he said in a low voice, "talk to that man again. Or allow our son anywhere near him."

His voice frightened her. "You're being ridiculous!"

"You will give your word," he ground out. "Or I'll never allow you to leave my sight again without six bodyguards at your side."

"You won't *allow* me?" she cried.

His jaw clenched. "It's a dangerous world. I have enemies. Luigi has good cause to hate me and he could choose to take it out on you. Or our child."

"How can you think of the world like that?"

"Because that's how it is," he said grimly.

Hallie stared at him in horror. He was refusing to even consider that he might be wrong about Luigi. Justifying his own selfish actions by trying to punish a sweet old man who hadn't done anything wrong.

"It's not true." The lump in her throat became a razor blade as she whispered, "The world is full of second chances. It's full of love if you only—"

Still cradling their sleeping baby, Cristiano turned away. "I'm done talking." He looked at his platinum watch. "I'll take Jack upstairs to Agata. Go get ready for the gala."

"Why are you acting like this?" she whispered.

"It's my responsibility to protect my family."

"But not to tell us anything." Anger filled her. "Agata told me that we're leaving Italy tomorrow."

He looked off-kilter. "She told you?"

"Did you think I wouldn't notice when she started packing all our clothes?"

"Yes. We're leaving for Tokyo." He lifted a dark eyebrow. "So?"

Swallowing over the pain in her throat, she choked out, "You said this was our home."

"And the next place will be, as well. And the place after that."

Hallie stared at him. "You spent millions on this villa, just for us to live here a few weeks?"

"And if I did?" he said coolly. "I can buy you ten more houses anywhere around the world. I can always sell them again. What does it matter?"

Hallie looked at him, stricken. "You said we'd have a home. You said we'd be a family."

"And we are. But we're doing it my way."

"And your way is to drag us around the world

at your beck and call, and tell me who I can and cannot speak with?"

Holding their baby against his chest, Cristiano set his jaw. "Either you're with me, or against me. Either you're my partner—"

"Your prisoner!" she cried.

"Or you're my enemy." His eyes glittered. "Decide carefully, *cara mia*, who you want to be. Now get ready." He gave her an icy smile. "You must sparkle like a star tonight."

And he left her.

Numb with shock, Hallie went back into the salon. She collected the red Cinderella dress. But as she carried it upstairs, it felt heavy in her arms.

As she got ready that night, putting on exquisite lingerie and the gorgeous designer ball gown, she felt cold inside. She brushed her dark hair until it shone, then stopped, looking at herself in the mirror.

When she tried to defy him, to fight for their happiness, he saw her as an enemy instead of recognizing it for what it was—love.

How could it be otherwise, when he'd never known what it was to be really, truly loved by another?

Either you're with me, or against me.

How could she get through his darkness, the pain of his childhood that still enveloped him like a shroud?

How could she show him that the world was more than danger and betrayal and cruelty and regret? Could she show him that she wasn't his enemy, but that she was fighting for his happiness, as well as her own?

Cristiano had given them his name, his wealth, his status. But Hallie and their son would never be more than possessions to him. He would never give them a home. Unless…

She took a deep breath.

There was only one way to break through. One risk she had to take, to win or lose it all.

Putting on lipstick, Hallie met her own scared eyes in the mirror.

Tonight she would tell him she loved him.

CHAPTER EIGHT

WEARING HIS TUXEDO, Cristiano paced furiously at the bottom of the villa's sweeping stairs. They were already five minutes late to his own hotel's grand opening gala.

Another transgression to add to the list. A low curse escaped his lips.

He could not believe Hallie had gone behind his back to speak to his father, his mortal enemy.

He'd thought he could trust her. Their marriage had been going so well. Living in this lavish villa overlooking the sea, as he'd been busy overseeing the Campania Cavello's final preparations, Hallie had been the perfect wife: beautiful, patient, supportive and uncomplaining. She'd been an excellent mother to their son by day and a hot temptress in Cristiano's bed by night. In his opinion, it was the perfect relationship.

Then she'd snuck out to meet Luigi Bennato behind his back.

Cristiano ground his teeth. He would send Salvatore to visit the man and warn him off. No, better yet, he'd send a lawyer. Send a cease-and-desist letter. Get a restraining order. Yes. Then he'd take Hallie, leave Italy and never return.

But the world was a small place. What would stop Bennato from contacting Hallie again if she wanted it? Pacing, he clawed his hand through his dark hair.

If Hallie wouldn't obey his rules, how could he protect her? How could he keep Hallie and the baby safe? How could he make sure he never lost them?

His eyes narrowed. He hoped she now realized the error of her ways. He expected her to apologize tonight. He would try to forgive her.

He would also make sure she never had the chance to betray him again.

"Am I late?" He heard her sweet voice from behind him.

Turning, Cristiano looked up and sucked in his breath.

Hallie was at the top of the stairs, her glossy hair pulled up in an elegant bun. Her red ball gown fit perfectly, from the tight bodice to the full skirts. He held his breath as he watched her come down the stairs, in awe at her beauty.

"You are magnificent," he said in a low voice. She smiled, her cheeks turning a pretty shade of pink.

"You are too kind." But she gave him a troubled glance from beneath her dark lashes. Her lips were full and red. His eyes widened, then fell lower to the round curve of her breasts, plump and ripe beneath the corset-style bodice.

Even as angry as he was, he was tempted to grab her and take her back upstairs. He'd already started to reach for her when he caught himself. He couldn't miss the gala tonight. He was the host. He took a deep breath and forced himself to pretend he was civilized.

"I have something for you, *cara*. The perfect addition to your dress."

Reaching into his tuxedo jacket pocket, he pulled out a flat black velvet box. Inside it was a sparkling diamond necklace. As she gasped, he put it gently around her neck, attaching the clasp at the back.

Hallie looked down at the glittering stones. "They're beautiful."

"Nothing compared to you, my beautiful wife," he whispered, kissing her. Feeling her lips against his was pure heaven, making him tremble with the power of her unconscious sensuality. When he finally drew back, he was more determined than ever to make her submit to his will, to keep their perfect marriage exactly as it was.

He held out his arm. "Shall we go?"

She hesitated, then took his arm, wrapping her hands around the sleeve of his black tuxedo jacket.

After helping her into his red sports car, he drove the short distance to the new Campania Hotel Cavello, clinging to a rocky cliff overlooking the village across the bay. A uniformed valet took their car, and they walked into the hotel on a red carpet. She clung to his arm as photographers flashed pictures of them. "Look over here!"

"*Signora!*"

"Mrs. Moretti!"

Hallie didn't exhale until they were inside. Then her eyes widened as she breathed, "Wow."

She looked around the lobby of his new hotel. The Campania Cavello made up for its boutique size by the lavishness of its furnishings and incredible view. Seeing the awe on Hallie's face, Cristiano felt his heart swell with pride.

"And this is just the lobby," he said, putting his hand over hers. "Wait until you see the ballroom."

Joining the other illustrious, glamorous guests,

he led her into the gilded ballroom. She stared up at the high ceilings, the bright mirrors, the chandeliers. Multiple French doors opened straight onto an expansive terrace, decked with bright pink flowers, and, beyond that, the moonlit sea.

Whirling back to face him, she breathed, "This place is amazing." Her head suddenly craned. "Is that Nadia Cruz?"

Cristiano shrugged as the famous Spanish actress, now married to a duke, walked by in a tight dress. He had eyes for only one woman. He wanted her in his arms. Against his body. In his bed.

But the object of the evening was to celebrate the grand opening of the hotel with the celebrities who would be his future guests. Any hotel, no matter how exquisite, depended upon publicity from a certain type of clientele to make the property popular amongst the glitterati.

So for the next hour, he forced himself to greet powerful guests with all the force of his charm. He gave them his complete attention, until the new hotel's manager privately informed him they were already booked up through Christmas, and the red-carpet arrivals had drawn attention from the press worldwide.

The Campania Cavello was a smashing success.

As soon as the music began, Cristiano took Hallie's hand. "Dance with me."

She looked around nervously at all the famous people in the ballroom. "We should let someone else go first."

"No one," he said arrogantly, "would dare."

Holding her hand tightly, he led her to the center of the ballroom floor. He felt the eyes of all the guests on him, heard their whispered comments, and he knew that every man here envied him to-night. Not for his money or power—for the beautiful woman in his arms.

He'd been envied before, as a well-known play-boy, a free-spirited billionaire who traveled the world, never settling down in any place or with any person.

This was different. Successful beyond imagination, he was now also married to a beautiful woman who'd been untouched by any other man. She'd not only given him the best sex of his life, she'd given him a son, an heir to carry on his line. Cristiano's future was secure.

He deserved to be envied.

As they danced, Cristiano looked around the gilded ballroom of the lavish Amalfi Coast hotel.

This was his. Cristiano's hands tightened on Hallie. And so was she.

He'd come a long way from hardscrabble poverty in Naples, when he'd been unwanted, unloved and often hungry and dirty. His parents hadn't wanted him. His mother had resented him; his father had abandoned him.

Now he had a new family.

From the beginning, when he'd first charmed that rich widow in Rome into selling her *palazzo* for a song, Cristiano's charm had been his second-greatest asset.

The first, of course, was his ruthlessness.

I've conquered the past completely, he thought. *I've won.*

Dancing with Hallie, he couldn't take his eyes off her.

"You are so beautiful," he said huskily, swaying her in his arms. "Every man here wishes he could be in my place."

"To own this hotel."

"To be in your bed."

She glanced around shyly. "Don't be silly."

"You have no idea how desirable you are," he whispered against her cheek, leaning forward. "Later tonight, you can apologize for that foolishness with Bennato," he murmured lazily, running his hand down her back. "And I will forgive you. Because I can deny you nothing."

"I'm not sorry," she said.

With an intake of breath, Cristiano looked down at her.

"Because I did it for a good reason." Her caramel-brown eyes were feverishly bright.

"What is that?" he said coldly.

Her red, luscious lips curved in a tremulous smile.

"Because I love you," she whispered.

For a few seconds, frozen on the dance floor, he stared at her as couples continued to whirl around them.

"You love me," he said slowly.

"Yes." Hallie's face was deliriously happy. "I know it wasn't supposed to happen. But it has. I love you, Cristiano. For the boy you were. The man you are. The man you'll be."

The boy you were.

Hallie's words felt like ice in his heart. She saw past his defenses? Past all his wealth and power, to see the helpless boy he'd once been?

His hands tightened on her.

"I love you," she choked out, searching his

gaze desperately. "I'm not your enemy. And I'm not your servant. I'm your wife. I'm fighting for our family. For our home. I'm fighting for you… because I love you."

Music swelled around them in the ballroom. A warm sea breeze blew in from doors opened wide to the moonlit terrace.

Hallie *loved* him.

How could she?

Then he got it.

A low, fierce laugh bubbled up from inside him as he realized what she was doing. He relaxed instantly.

"What's so funny?"

"Nothing," he said, still laughing. He shook his head admiringly. "I just respect you."

"You *respect* me?"

"Yes." He sometimes thought that women didn't realize how valuable it was, respect. Most men he knew could tolerate a lack of love far better than any lack of respect. But the women he'd known in his life, starting with his mother, seemed to feel the opposite, willing to put up with a total lack of respect from their lovers, finding it acceptable to be taken for granted and talked down to, as long as they were loved. He'd never understood that.

Hallie clearly didn't see his perspective, either. Her deep brown eyes looked hurt. "That's all you have to say?"

"I don't blame you for trying. You thought that angle might work. But it will take more than that to manipulate me."

Her beautiful face was pale. "You think that's what I was trying to do? Manipulate you?"

"Of course it is." Leaning down, he confided, "You're wasting your time. That emotional stuff doesn't work on me, but—" reaching down, he twisted a tendril of her hair "—you're welcome to try to convince me in bed. Not that it will work, but we'll both enjoy it."

Angrily she pulled her head away. "I'm telling you the truth!"

"Fine." He rolled his eyes. She seemed determined to stick with her story. "But there will be no more complaining. We will never stop traveling. We will never settle in just one place. And if you ever speak to Bennato again—" he looked at her evenly "—I will divorce you."

Her brown eyes were cold. "You would divorce me? Just for talking to someone?"

Cristiano would have thought it obvious. "For talking to my enemy."

Men in tuxedos and women in bright, sparkling gowns continued to dance around them, in a ballroom lit by gilded chandeliers and flooded with silvery moonlight.

"That's how the world is to you, isn't it?" Hallie said slowly. "Either a person is your enemy or your slave." Her eyes were huge as she whispered, "You're never going to change, are you?"

His expression hardened. "Hallie—"

"No!"

She ripped her arm away, leaving him alone on the ballroom floor. His illustrious guests were now staring at him with big eyes and rising glee. Of course. The only thing people liked better than heroes with enviable lives was seeing those lives fall apart spectacularly.

Turning, he followed his wife out of the hotel.

She was already halfway up the twisting street, climbing the hill. She meant to walk the mile back to the villa, he realized. Even in that impractical red ball gown and high heels. Most of the paparazzi had gone, but a scruffy-looking photographer was following a few feet behind her, peppering her with questions.

Cristiano's whole body felt tight as he turned to the valet. "My Ferrari."

The young valet got his car back in thirty seconds. Jumping into the sports car, Cristiano roared along the street and quickly caught up with her. He rolled down the window.

"Get in the car," he barked. "Now."

Hallie didn't even look in his direction. She just kept climbing up the steep road in her high heels and red ball gown.

By now, the photographer had backed off and was simply taking pictures of them both. Cristiano ground his teeth. He had no doubt that the celebrity gossip sites would be full of stories about "Trouble in Paradise" tomorrow.

"Now," he ordered.

She tripped on a rock, nearly twisting her ankle. Muttering under his breath, he pulled over, blocking her path with his car. Still not looking at him, she climbed in, slamming the door behind her. Without a word, he pressed on the gas, and the powerful engine leaped forward with a roar.

Everything seemed to have changed between them. She remained silent, seeming fragile, brittle. A side of her he'd never seen before.

The pleasurable night, which had seemed so bright and delicious, was suddenly lost. Entering the security code at the gate, he drove up the sweeping drive. The villa was frosted by the opalescent moon in the dark, velvety sky.

After pulling the car into the separate six-car garage, he turned off the engine. They both sat for a moment in silence. Then Hallie turned to him with sudden desperation.

"Could you ever love me? Could you?"

It was a serious question. He looked at her across the car. She hadn't been trying to manipulate him, after all. She actually believed she loved him.

The thought chilled him to the bone. He had the sudden memory of himself as a boy, hungry and cold and pathetically desperate for love. Crying for it.

He'd never feel that way again.

"No," he said quietly. "I will never love you. Or anyone."

Her face became a sickly green. She turned to open her door. Stumbling out of the car, she rushed from the garage and onto the driveway, red skirts flying behind her.

"Hallie, wait," he said tersely, slamming the car door behind him.

She didn't slow down. She fled toward the villa's gardens overlooking the sea, the skirt of her red dress flying behind her, a slash of scarlet in the moonlight.

He followed, reaching her at the hedge maze, with the eight-foot-tall, sharply cut hedges towering above them, luring them into the shadows of the green labyrinth.

"Hallie, damn you! Stop!"

Grasping her arm, he twisted her around, pressing her back against the hedge.

"Let me go," she panted, struggling. "You—are a *liar*!"

Her breath came in hot, quick gasps. His lips parted to argue, but as he looked from the fury in her eyes to the quick pant of her full breasts, pushing up against the strapless bodice of her dress, desire overwhelmed him. He tried to kiss her.

For the first time, Hallie turned her head away so he could not.

Cristiano stared down at her with narrowed eyes, his own heart suddenly pounding with anger at her rejection.

"I never asked for your love," he ground out. "I never wanted it."

She lifted her chin, and her eyes glittered in the moonlight. "No. You just want to possess me. You want my body. Not my heart."

Silence fell, with the only sound the angry pant of her breath. His gaze again fell to her sweetly seductive mouth. Her pink tongue licked the corners of her red lips.

"Love me if you want. I don't care." He looked down at her. "But you will obey me."

"*Obey* you?" She gave a harsh laugh. "This isn't the Middle Ages. I am not your property. And I never will be."

"Aren't you?" He breathed in the scent of her, like vanilla and summer flowers. Her skin beneath his grasp felt hot to the touch. Her dark eyes sucked him into fury and despair, all tangled up in wanton, desperate desire.

Gripping her wrists against the hedge, Cristiano lowered his head roughly to hers.

He did it to prove a point. To master her. But as he kissed her, as her struggles ended and he felt her surrender, when he felt her desire rise against him like a tide, he too was suddenly lost.

I love you, she'd said. *I am not your property.*

Kissing her, he was dizzy with need. He wanted to take her right here, right now, in the moonlight and shadows of the labyrinth.

Hallie wrenched away. "Don't touch me," she whispered harshly.

He stared down at her in shock. Without her in his arms, he felt suddenly bereft. Rejected. *Vulnerable*.

The one feeling he'd vowed he'd never feel again.

Rage exploded inside him. He let it build until it was all encompassing, blocking out any other emotion.

Looking down at his wife, he narrowed his eyes and spoke the words he knew would hurt her more than any others.

"You want me to tell you I love you, Hallie? Fine," Cristiano said coldly. "I love you."

Hallie stared up at him, her heart in her throat.

He loved her?

Trembling, she stumbled back a step into the shadows of the hedge maze. She whispered, "You do?"

"Want me to be more convincing?" Coming closer, he kissed her cheek, her lips, her throat. "I love you, *cara mia*," he whispered. "I love you. *Ti amo*."

And she heard the mockery behind his words.

Tearfully she said, "I didn't know you had such cruelty in you!"

"Did you not?" he said, looking devastatingly handsome and cold as marble in his perfectly cut tuxedo. "Then you chose to be blind."

Hallie felt like crying. The way he'd looked at her at the gala had made her bold. It had made her brave. All her instincts had told her that if she took the risk, if she told him she loved him, she could rescue him from his dark past.

Her instincts had been wrong.

Now, standing in her red dress in the shadowy hedge maze, she felt like she was in a Gothic Victorian nightmare. Knowing he didn't love her back was heartbreaking, but she might have been able to endure it as long as she had hope that, someday, perhaps he could.

Cristiano had taken even that hope away from her, and then used her own words of love to mock her. He'd made it clear that their marriage would be on his terms alone.

She was to fill his bed and raise his child, and he would give her nothing in return. Not his heart. Not his love.

Not even a home.

She wiped her eyes. "You heartless bastard," she whispered. "What have you done to me?"

"Now it's my fault, because I cannot return the

love I never asked you to feel?" He looked down at her icily. "I do not have the ability to produce feelings on command. What you want from me, I cannot give."

Pain ripped through her and, along with it, the humiliating realization that for all his coldness and cruelty, she loved him. Still.

"What will we do?" she whispered.

"Our marriage will continue as always."

Her eyes widened. "Are you serious?"

"Nothing has changed between us. We leave for Tokyo in the morning."

Hallie didn't realize her knees had buckled beneath her until he was beside her, supporting her arm.

"It's late, Hallie," he said quietly. "You're tired. Come inside."

She looked up at him wordlessly as he half carried her into the villa. Inside, it was dark and quiet. The rooms were elegant and empty. They seemed to go on forever.

On the second floor, they found Agata sitting outside the nursery, knitting. The older woman looked between them, then said only, "The baby had a good night. He just fell asleep."

In the darkened nursery, Hallie looked down at

her sleeping baby. Jack's fat arms stretched back above his head. His chubby cheeks moved as his mouth pursed in his sleep.

Coming behind her, Cristiano put his hands heavily on her shoulders, his voice firm. "Let's put our quarrel behind us, Hallie. This is what's important." He looked down at the crib. "Our son. Our family."

A lump rose in Hallie's throat.

He was right. Family was the most important thing to her. For years, all she'd tried to do was recapture what she'd lost. To have a family again. A home.

How had it all gone so wrong? A lifetime in a loveless marriage stretched ahead of her. Instead of having a home, surrounded by friends, at her husband's command she would be forced to travel from hotel to hotel.

Her hands tightened at her sides. And her son would be raised to think this was *normal*. He'd see the cold relationship between his parents and think it was what marriage was. What *family* was. He'd never know what a family was meant to be—a rowdy, chaotic life of give and take, of arguing and joking and kisses, filled with love.

Her tiny baby's soul would be warped by this, just as Cristiano's had once been.

With an intake of breath, Hallie looked up.

Cristiano frowned when he saw her expression. "What is it?"

She'd thought commitment made a home. That was why she'd married him. She'd thought, if she took his name, if they lived under the same roof, under his protection, they'd be a family.

But there was a reason that, in spite of all his money and lavish gifts, Hallie hadn't felt as happy and secure as she had as a child. A reason, even in this amazing, luxurious villa, she'd never truly felt at home.

"Love makes a family," she breathed. "Love makes a home."

Certainty rushed through her, clanging like a bell. Her husband had said he would never love her. He would never take that risk. He would never give up anything he couldn't afford to lose. He would never give himself.

Hallie's heart tightened. Her back snapped straight.

Turning on her heel, she went to the enormous master bedroom. She took a suitcase from the shelf of the walk-in closet.

Cristiano's voice came from the doorway. "What do you think you're doing?"

There wasn't much to take. She didn't need all the expensive designer clothes, not anymore. And she'd left her family treasures back in New York. Along with her friends.

She looked at him.

"I'm going home."

"Home," he scoffed.

"New York." Saying the name aloud made her realize how desperate she was to return. "I'm going home to the people who love me."

She turned back to the closet, then stopped. He'd bought her so much, but what did she actually need? Nothing. She didn't want anything he'd bought her. Because he hadn't been buying her clothes. He'd been buying her soul. Telling her how she had to behave and where she would live and who she would be.

Looking down at herself, she couldn't bear for the beautiful red ball gown to be touching her skin. It reminded her of how naive she'd been, to believe she could just tell him she loved him and magically change him, like some fairy tale!

Reaching back, she savagely yanked on the zipper, pulling off the dress and kicking it away from her body. She stood in front of him, wearing only a white lace bra and panties and the cold diamond necklace on her throat.

"Hallie, don't do anything foolish."

"You don't believe in love. You don't believe in home." Reaching up, she pulled off the glittering diamond necklace and held it out, a hard heap of metal and stone. "Take it back."

When he didn't move, she opened her hand, letting it drop heavily to the floor. Turning away, she dug through the closet until she found one of her old cotton sundresses. Pulling it over her body, she left the closet, carrying the empty suitcase.

"Go, then," he growled.

Stopping by the enormous bed where he'd once given her such joy, she whirled to face him. His eyes were black.

"Go off in search of this imaginary man who will feel whatever you want him to feel, whenever you want it, trained on your command like a barking dog."

She took a deep breath, her heart full of anguish. "That's not what I—"

"*You* can go," he interrupted. He paused. "My son stays."

Hallie's mouth went dry.

"What?" she croaked.

Her husband's dark eyes glittered as his cruel, sensual lips curved. "You heard me."

"You would take him from me?" she whispered. "From his own mother?"

"You are the one abandoning him, if you leave. And, as I warned you from the beginning, he is my priority. Not you."

His words stabbed her in the heart. "But—but you're hardly ever home! You spend all your time working. You'd rather see Jack raised by some paid nanny?" She lifted her chin. "I don't care what you say, no judge would agree to that!"

Cristiano tilted his head. "It seems you didn't read our prenuptial agreement carefully, *cara*. In the event of a divorce, unless I am in breach of our agreement, primary custody goes to me." He smiled. "You are, of course, welcome to visit Jack whenever you wish."

His voice was silky, as if he knew he'd just beaten her. And he had. She staggered back, unable to believe that the man she loved could be so cold and unforgiving.

"You bastard," she whispered.

"Me?" His eyes suddenly blazed. "I've done everything for you, Hallie," he ground out. "Everything. I've given you everything any woman could possibly desire. I bought you this house—"

"Because you wanted revenge against your father! Nothing to do with me!"

"This house was for you. Hurting Bennato was just a bonus. And yet you still decided to go behind my back and try to help him infiltrate our family."

"He never meant to abandon you! Why won't you even talk to him?"

"Because he would say anything to try to hurt me. And, at the moment, so would you."

That made Hallie gasp. "Do you really believe that?"

"You're either with me or against me."

Searching his gaze, she choked out, "Are you trying to make me hate you?"

"Perhaps. At least hate," Cristiano said softly, tucking back a tendril of her hair, "is an emotion I believe in."

They were so close, facing each other in the luxurious bedroom, next to the enormous four-poster bed. Beyond that, the French doors opened to the terrace on the edge of the sea.

Hallie looked up at her husband. The powerful, sexy billionaire that every other woman wanted.

To the outside world, she knew it seemed as if she had everything any woman could ever want.

But he was so damaged inside, the truth was she had nothing at all.

She said, "I won't let you take my baby away."

"I won't have to." He gave her a hard smile. "Because you're not going anywhere. We will remain one big happy family. You will remain at my side. In my bed. Bearing my children."

"Children?" Her voice was strangled.

He lifted an eyebrow. "We will have other children," he said mildly. "Surely you would not want Jack to be alone?"

It was the final straw. Closing her eyes, Hallie took a deep breath.

She knew what she had to do. The thought turned her heart to ice. It wasn't what she wanted.

But he'd left her no choice.

"I'm done arguing about this," Cristiano said. "You will be happy, as you were before. You will appreciate what I can give you and ignore what I cannot." Reaching out, he cupped her cheek.

Opening her eyes, she spoke, her voice clear and unflinching. "You missed dinner with us this week."

He frowned. "What?"

"Twice. You were gone from dawn till midnight. You didn't share a single meal with us on those days, as Agata and other staff members can attest."

His shoulders were suddenly tense. He knew what she meant. Dropping his hand, he said defensively, "I was working at the hotel—"

"It doesn't matter. You failed to uphold my rules. So you're in breach of our agreement," she said, stepping back.

Her husband stared at her, his dark eyes wide. His lips parted to speak and closed again.

He looked vulnerable. Shaken.

Hallie forced herself not to care, to treat him exactly as he'd treated her.

"As you're in breach of the prenup, I will get primary custody. So I'm taking Jack with me to New York. Please feel free," she added lightly, in the same tone he'd used, "to visit whenever you want."

Cristiano stared at her in shock, not moving.

No. Hallie blocked the pain from her heart. She wasn't going to feel anything. She wasn't going to let him push her around ever again.

She turned away, dragging the suitcase behind her. Stopping at the door, she faced him one last time across the shadowy bedroom where they'd once set the world on fire.

"Thank you, Cristiano." Her voice echoed between them as she said flatly, "Thank you for teaching me how the world really is."

And she left.

CHAPTER NINE

"SIGNOR." LOOKING UP from where he'd been pacing the hotel's terrace just after dawn, Cristiano saw Luca Pizzati, the new manager. The young man gave him an apologetic smile. "Sir, you are acting crazy. The entire staff is threatening to quit."

Cristiano's mouth fell open. How could the man say such a thing?

The day after his wife and child left him, Cristiano had planned to leave for Tokyo. And after that, Seoul. And after that… Cristiano couldn't remember. But he'd been forced to stay in Cavello. Something wasn't right here, and until he could find the source of the problem, he couldn't leave. He could barely eat or sleep. All he could do was pace the halls of the hotel, checking every detail, trying to find the problem that haunted him, taunted him, just out of his reach.

"Look at this," Cristiano ground out. He yanked a purple flower from a bougainvillea bush that was a slightly different shade from the rest. "A disgrace! Do I have to fix everything?"

The young manager looked at the flower, then Cristiano.

"Signor Moretti," he said gently, "when was the last time you slept?"

He bit out furiously, "How can I sleep, until the hotel is perfect?"

"It will never be perfect," the manager said. "Because people are living in it."

Cristiano took a deep breath. Blinking hard, he looked up at the beautiful new hotel. It was already full of guests and getting nothing but praise. He looked down at the flower in his hand. He'd been about to scream at the gardening staff because the bougainvillea flowers were not all the exact same shade of purple.

Pizzati was right. He *was* acting crazy.

Crushing the bloom in his fingers, Cristiano tossed it to the ground.

"You're right," he said in a low voice. "Please give the staff my apologies. I… I will stop."

The manager came closer, a look of concern in his eyes. "Shall I send for your driver? Or would you like Esposito to take you home?"

The empty villa was the last place Cristiano

wanted to be. There, he heard only the echoes of his baby son's laughter in the nursery, of his wife's sweet singing in the garden. And in the bedroom, the haunting echo of her soft moans from the times he'd made love to her.

Lost, all lost.

And he was tired. So tired. Thinking of his wife and child, a strange ice spread slowly through Cristiano's body, down his neck, to his spine, until his fingers and toes felt numb. At that point he felt nothing, absolutely nothing.

"Sir?"

He focused with effort. Then he nodded heavily. "Thank you, Mr. Pizzati. I leave the hotel in good hands. Please order my pilot to ready the plane for Tokyo."

"Of course, sir." The manager sounded relieved. Cristiano could only imagine how many problems he'd caused the man over the last ten days.

He tried to remember what his scheduled meetings in Asia were about. Marcia had left him multiple messages, as had various board members, all of which he'd ignored. He took a deep breath. He pictured the Campania Hotel Tokyo, ultramodern and gleaming in the Shinjuku district.

But when he tried to recall the details, all he

could remember was the darkness in his wife's eyes the night she'd left him.

Thank you for teaching me how the world really is.

"Have a pleasant trip, sir," the manager said.

Turning, Cristiano left the terrace without a word. When he came out of the lobby into the bright Italian sunshine, Marco was waiting to take him back home.

Home. The word tasted bitter on his tongue. There was no such thing. It was a lie. A dream. Like love.

As the Rolls-Royce passed through the gate one last time, he looked up at the magnificent nineteenth-century villa. He wished he'd never come here. He'd done it to prove that he'd triumphed over his past.

Instead, it had triumphed over him.

When Hallie had told him she loved him, he should have said the words back to her and made her believe them. Why hadn't he tried? It would have been a lie, but at least their marriage would have endured. She would never have known the difference.

Why, instead, had he mocked her, then told her

the truth—that he didn't have the ability to love her or anyone? Was it pride?

Or had he just wanted one person on earth to really, truly know who he was deep inside? A man so flawed that he didn't know what love was, or home?

But he did know one thing.

He looked at Luigi Bennato's spectacular villa, clinging to the cliffs above the bright blue sea.

He was done with this place. He would put it on the market at once.

An hour later, after the staff had packed his clothes, he was on the way to a private airport twenty minutes inland.

Cristiano stared out of the sedan's back seat window, not noticing the palm trees or tiny stone churches or lush groves of lemon trees.

He wondered how Hallie was enjoying New York. Was she happy? How was the baby?

Was Hallie already looking for a new home? A new love?

His stomach twisted.

He'd heard she'd signed some kind of record deal with a top executive at an independent label in New York, the man who'd casually given her that card in Rome. Life could be like that. One chance meeting could change your life.

Like coming home early to find a beautiful maid singing in his penthouse while she changed the sheets of his bed.

Clarence Loggia, the manager of the Campania New York, had called Cristiano last night to tell him that Hallie's agent had arranged for her to make her big debut tonight at the Blue Hour, the hotel's jazz club.

"I assume you approve," Clarence had said delicately.

His wife? Appearing on stage, singing for strangers, while Cristiano was on the other side of the ocean? No way. He wanted her to sing only for him, like a songbird in a cage.

Closing her eyes, he'd thought of Hallie's sweet, haunting voice. Her songs of longing and heartbreak. Love. Home. Family.

"No..." Cristiano had started, but he forced himself to finish, "No problem. Tell the club's manager to give her everything she needs. The best time slot, good lighting, advertising. Everything."

"Of course, Signor Moretti." He'd paused. "You will be there, no?"

"No," Cristiano had replied, and he'd hung up.

He wondered how Hallie was feeling right before her New York debut. Was she scared? Would the audience appreciate her, as she deserved? Would they realize what a gift she was to them?

Staring out the window, he saw they were passing an old shack he knew, even though he'd never been there.

There was only one way to put the past behind him. Only one way to truly triumph over it, once and for all. And it had nothing to do with money.

You'll never talk to him, will you? You hate him beyond all reason. You'll never be free.

"Stop," he said.

His driver looked confused but obligingly pulled over into a gravel drive on the side of the road.

"Wait here," he told Marco and Salvatore.

Outside, as he shut the sedan door behind him, he could hear the roar of the sea beneath the cliff, hear the soft sway of palm trees in the hot summer wind, scented with sea salt and spices from across the Mediterranean.

His heart was pounding as he slowly went to the front door. *I'm afraid of nothing*, he told himself. He pounded on the door with his fist. He heard footsteps. Then it opened.

And Cristiano saw Luigi Bennato for the first time in fifteen years.

The man looked bowed, gray. A shadow of the boisterous, vital man he remembered. Had time done this? he wondered. Or had it been his betrayal?

Seeing him, Luigi's dark eyes widened. Suddenly life and color came back into the old man's pale cheeks. "Cristiano?"

"I'm giving you back your villa," he said tersely. "It's yours. Keep it. Just never contact me or my family again."

Hands clenching at his sides, he turned away.

"No," the old man said.

Cristiano stopped, turning around in shock. "What?"

The gray-haired man looked at him. "I don't need a villa. What I need," he whispered, "is a son."

"You should have thought of that before you tried to force my mother to get rid of me when she was pregnant," he said, "then tossed her out on the street."

"All I did was keep her from drinking while she was pregnant. And she hated me for it."

"Why would you do that?"

"Because from the moment Violetta told me she was pregnant, I loved you."

The wind blew softly against Cristiano's face. From a distance, he could hear traffic on the road, the cry of seagulls.

"That's a lie," he said in a low voice.

"You know how she was. You know better than anyone," he said sadly. "Violetta was beautiful. Charming. But so broken. She accused me of keeping her prisoner. A few months before you were born, she disappeared without a trace."

Cristiano thought of his mother's fury if anyone tried to take her alcohol away. Once, when he was nine, he'd dared to pour out her bottles of whiskey while she was passed out. She'd slapped him so hard his ears rang for weeks.

"You made her a drunk."

"I did?" Luigi slowly shook his head. "We met in a bar, when she offered to buy me a drink. I'd never seen any woman hold her liquor so well. Stupidly, I was impressed."

That made sense to Cristiano, too. Agata had told him that when she worked for Bennato, the man had rarely touched alcohol. He took a deep breath.

"If you knew I existed, and you claim to care,"

he said slowly, "why didn't you keep trying to find me?"

"I did. For years," the old man choked out. He blinked fast, shaking his head. Tears streamed down his wrinkled cheeks. "But you're right," he whispered. "I should have looked harder. It wasn't until I saw her picture in the paper, a few days after she died, that I knew where you were. But before I could leave for Naples, you showed up at my hotel in Capri, asking for a job. I thought it was a miracle. I thought it was my chance."

"Why didn't you say anything?"

"I told myself I needed proof first. But the truth was... I was afraid." He swallowed. "After the way Violetta raised you, why would you ever forgive me? I was a coward. And I waited too long. By the time I had proof you were my son, you'd already left. And I didn't want to cause you more pain."

"I betrayed you."

"I didn't see it as a betrayal."

"How did you see it?"

The elderly man whispered, "Justice."

A tear slid down his wrinkled cheek.

Cristiano stared down at him in shock. Everything was different than he'd imagined. Everything.

"Can you ever forgive me?" Luigi choked out. He reached his shaking hand to Cristiano's shoulder. "I loved you so much. But I could not protect you. I failed."

Cristiano stood frozen in front of the old wooden shack. The sun felt too bright on his face. Clenching his jaw, he looked out at the sea.

Hallie had tried to tell him. She'd tried to save him from his own darkness.

"So you just let me destroy you," Cristiano said slowly. "You let me take everything from you, and make it mine."

"Of course I did," Luigi said quietly. "You're my son. Your happiness means more to me than my own. I love you."

Cristiano heard the echo of Hallie's voice.

Love makes a family. Love makes a home.

"My mother said you abandoned us," he said. "After she died, I wanted to make you suffer."

"It's not your fault, my son," Luigi said hoarsely. "I should have taken you into my arms the day you walked into my hotel. I should have—"

With a sob, Luigi pulled him into his arms.

For a moment, Cristiano stiffened.

"So much time has been lost," Luigi whispered, hugging him. "Because I was afraid. Because I was ashamed. Years we can never get back. Oh, my son. Can you forgive me?"

So much time has been lost.

Still held in his father's arms, Cristiano thought of the ten days he'd been separated from his wife and child. Ten days had felt like eternity, driving him half-mad.

What if they were separated for a lifetime? Until he, too, was apologizing for his cowardice and shame?

He gasped, and suddenly realized he was hugging his father back. Hearing Luigi's sobs of joy, Cristiano's heart cracked in his chest.

Emotions suddenly poured through him. Grief and anguish and every other feeling he'd blocked for years. Everything he hadn't let himself feel.

And love.

Love so big it seemed to be exploding out of his body with light brighter than the sun.

As he stood in a little village on the edge of the Amalfi Coast, hugged by his father for the very first time, Cristiano took a deep breath. Even the air seemed different in his lungs.

"Thank you for that," Luigi said, finally releasing him. He wiped his eyes. "You've made an old man so happy."

As Cristiano stared down at his father, everything became crystal clear.

Hallie.

Oh, God, how could he not have realized it before?

She was the one who'd tried to convince him to forgive his father. She'd loved Cristiano, even when he didn't deserve it. She'd seen the hurt and darkness inside him, and, instead of scorning him, she'd tried to heal it. She'd been brave enough to love him, flawed as he was.

He'd tossed it back in her face.

His spine snapped straight as he looked across the sea and realized, for the first time, exactly what love meant. What *family* meant.

Love didn't consume, like fire.

It gave, like the sun.

Cristiano took a deep breath and felt his shoulders expand as he sucked all the world into his lungs. His eyes narrowed in a private vow.

If she forgave him, he would show her that her faith in him hadn't been wrong.

He would give his wife, every single day on earth, a reason to sing.

"Cristiano?"

Eyes wide, Cristiano stumbled back from his father.

"I have to go find Hallie," he said. "I have to tell her…tell her…"

"Go." His father smiled at him through his tears. "And when you see her, please tell her something more. Tell her *thank you*."

"I can't do this," Hallie whispered.

"You can," Lola told her firmly. "I didn't go to all the trouble of getting dressed and leaving the house with a newborn just for you to back out at the last minute. You can do it."

From behind the Blue Hour's curtain, Hallie glanced out at the audience. "There are so many people."

"They'll love you. Look," Tess said. "I've got your biggest fan right here!"

Hallie smiled down at Jack, who was in a stroller next to Esme's, trying to grab his own chubby feet.

Hallie bit her lip as she looked out again from the wings of the jazz club's small stage. She would have preferred some out-of-the-way coffeehouse, with only five or six people in the audience. But her agent was no fool. He'd argued for Hallie to make her debut at the Blue Hour. "Why would you go anywhere else? You're married to Cristiano Moretti!"

Even for someone with half a million hits, the number of people who'd watched the YouTube video of her singing in Rome, it wasn't easy to perform in such an exclusive venue. So she'd told her agent to ask the manager, confident that when Cristiano heard about it he'd tell them all to go to hell.

But, apparently, he'd agreed.

Why was Cristiano being supportive of her career, when he'd made it clear he didn't give a damn about her?

It was a mystery.

Even after ten days, Hallie still couldn't believe he'd let them go so easily. Cristiano wasn't the kind of man to let himself be defeated, certainly not by some legal technicality. Why hadn't he come after her? Why hadn't he fought?

The answer had to be that he was secretly relieved to be rid of them.

She took a deep breath, looking down at the short black dress the music label's stylist had found for her. Tomorrow she was supposed to start work on an album, followed by a publicity tour. Once, this would have felt like a dream come true.

Now, it just felt like a job. A way to support her child so she wouldn't have to depend on a man who didn't love her.

The truth was that she didn't want to sing for strangers. She wanted to sing for the people she loved. For Cristiano. And she would have given it all up in a second if he'd come for her, to fight for her. For their family.

But he hadn't.

A jagged pain filled her throat. *Bad for singing*, she thought, and tried to think of happier things. She'd used some of that hundred-thousand-dollar check, which she'd tucked away in her savings account, to lease a one-bedroom walk-up apartment in the Lower East Side. But she was trying not to spend that. She wanted to save it for Jack's future, so she never had to ask Cristiano for anything ever again. Not even the alimony required by the prenuptial agreement. She hadn't filed for divorce. The mere thought of divorce filled her with blinding pain.

At the moment it felt like she was barely putting one foot ahead of the other. She didn't know how she would have survived without her friends.

"Stop that," Tess said, as she caught Lola yawning behind Hallie.

"I can't help it," the blonde said. "I only got four hours of sleep last night. Thanks to you," she said to her tiny baby with mock severity.

"Four hours isn't so bad," Tess said encouragingly. Lola rolled her eyes.

"One hour. Four times."

"Oh," Tess said, because there wasn't much good to say about that. Then she brightened. "But before you know it, your baby will be as big as Esme." She looked down at her five-month-old daughter, a dark-haired baby with adorable fat rolls on her thighs and bright emerald-green eyes.

"It's time," the stage manager called, and Hallie sucked in her breath.

Lola squeezed Hallie's shoulder. "I know you'll be great."

Tess gave her a sideways hug. "We'll be cheering for you!"

Then they left with the babies, and Hallie was alone. She heard the club's host announce, "And let's have a big Blue Hour welcome for debut artist... Hallie Hatfield!"

She'd left the Moretti name behind. The glamorous bride celebrated in the fashion blogs, the woman who'd brought the famous Cristiano Moretti to his knees—that obviously wasn't her. She was just Hallie, plain and simple.

Trembling, she went out on stage, in front of the house band. Beneath the spotlight, she couldn't see anyone in the audience, not even Tess or Lola or the babies. She gulped. She wasn't sure she could do this.

Then…

Closing her eyes, she focused on the music. The songs her mother and father had once sung to her, and her grandparents before.

Hallie's lips parted, and against her will she saw Cristiano's face. She sang directly to the man she loved. The man she'd lost.

Tears streamed down her cheeks as she sang of longing and heartbreak and regret. When she finally sang her last note, silence fell across the club.

Opening her eyes, Hallie looked out into the darkness beyond the spotlight. Had everyone left? Had they hated her songs and just gone home?

Then she heard it, sweeping across the club like a low roll of thunder.

A rush of applause built to shouts and cheers, lifting her sad heart. She smiled, overwhelmed with gratitude. She hadn't failed the audience who'd come to hear her, but still she felt sad.

"Thank you," she choked out. Wiping her tears, she stepped back from the microphone. As she turned away, she heard one man's voice above the rest.

"Hallie."

There was a collective intake of breath across the club. Turning back, she narrowed her eyes, trying to see who was calling to her. It sounded like…but it couldn't be…

The spotlight moved, and she saw him.

Her husband stood in the middle of the crowded jazz club, amid all the tables, his dark suit more rumpled than she'd ever seen it.

"Cristiano?" she breathed.

His dark eyes cut through her soul. Turning to the crowd, he held out his arm toward her. "Hallie is my wife." He spread his arms wide. "Have you ever heard such a voice?"

The audience applauded and hooted, stomping their feet. But Hallie had eyes only for him.

"What are you doing here?"

Cristiano's voice carried across the room as he turned to face her. "I don't need you, Hallie."

She sucked in her breath.

"At least that's what I told myself." He started walking past the crowded tables, toward the stage. "The truth was, I was afraid to need you." He stopped in front of the stage, staring up at her. "Because I was dead inside."

The club was so quiet you could have heard a pin drop.

"But you brought me to life." Cristiano smiled at her, his dark eyes shining. "It was your voice that caused the first crack in the wall around my heart. The first time I heard you sing. Do you remember?"

She nodded, a lump in her throat. How could she forget?

"I saw you, so vibrant and sexy and alive, and I knew from that moment that I had to have you. But it wasn't just your incredible voice that drew me. Not even your beautiful face and body. It was your soul, Hallie," he whispered. "Your heart."

By now, camera phones had appeared at every table, lighting up the club like candle flames, recording the moment as the famous billionaire Cristiano Moretti went onstage to join his wife.

"No." She struggled to speak. "I can't believe it."

"I spoke with my father," he said humbly. "And you were right. Everything you said. You were right."

Her heart was in her throat as she looked up at him.

"I know what love means now," he whispered. Then, to her shock, he fell to his knees on the stage in front of her. There was a gasp across the club.

Cristiano looked up at her. His eyes were vulnerable and raw. For the first time, the darkness was gone. For the first time, she truly saw his soul.

"Let me try to win back your heart. Let me show you I can be the man I was always meant to be." He took her hand in both of his. "I need you, Hallie," he whispered. "I love you."

Reaching down, she put her hand to his rough cheek in amazement. "You love me?"

He nodded, blinking back tears. "Tell me I'm not too late." His voice broke. "Tell me I still have the chance to be the man you deserve."

She pulled him to his feet. "The chance? No. You don't have a chance to win back my love."

Hallie smiled at him through her tears. "Because I never stopped loving you, Cristiano."

His handsome face filled with joy. Cupping her face in both his hands, he kissed her, long and hard. Hallie felt the flame spark between them, as always.

But something was different. Something was new. They knew each other now, really and truly. The fire burned bright and clear between them, in a blaze she knew would last forever.

Ignoring the applause and hoots from the audience, Cristiano looked down at her. "And you were right about something else."

"What?"

He gave her an impish grin. "The house you loved on Bank Street. The one you told me about. It does have a garden. And it was for sale, just like you said. I told my broker to put in an offer."

"What!"

"If you still want it," he amended. He searched her gaze. "Do you, *cara*?"

"Oh, Cristiano." Happy tears filled Hallie's eyes at the thought of having the home she'd dreamed of for all her life. "Do you really mean it? We can stay?"

"Forever, if you want." He cupped her cheek.

"Because you're not just my wife. You're my love song," he whispered. "My happiness, my heart-break and joy. You're my everything."

Looking down at her hand wrapped in his larger one, Hallie felt her heart in her throat.

"And you're mine." She looked up at him, blinking back tears. "From the moment you said you loved me, all my childhood dreams came true. We can live in New York, or anywhere in the world. Because now I know, for the rest of our lives," she breathed, her eyes shining with joy, "wherever we live, we're home."

* * * * *

LET'S TALK

Romance

For exclusive extracts, competitions
and special offers, find us online:

- **f** facebook.com/millsandboon
- **◎** @millsandboonuk
- **𝕐** @millsandboon

Or get in touch on 0844 844 1351*

For all the latest titles coming soon,
visit millsandboon.co.uk/nextmonth

*Calls cost 7p per minute plus your phone company's price per
minute access charge